AFTER SUNSET

a love story

Mary Ann Nocera

Publication date March 2013

This book is a work of fiction. Names, characters, places and incidents are a product of the author's imagination.

Cover design by author

ISBN-13: 978-0615782744
    Little Classics Publishing

ISBN-10: 0615782744

♥To my husband and sons♥

TABLE OF CONTENTS

Romance is defined as *"a strong, usually short-lived attachment of enthusiasm"…"a fictitiously embellished account or explanation"*

Love is defined as *"the person who is the object of such an attraction"…"beloved"…"deep affection and tenderness"…"for another."*

After Sunset *is a love story. This is a sensuous story of love and grief.*

One is fighting to live in the past, the other fighting to break that hold.

Spiritual—Real—Imagined—All of these.

Is this hold so strong they will be compelled to say goodbye?

PROLOGUE

♥

Sunset was a shrouded memory. Soft twilight had become dusk. The night was without light, no stars or moon. Large old oaks and maples, soon to be in leaf lined the narrow road. With familiarity the small blue car was traveling southbound. The music of Barber's *Adagio for Strings* softly filled the otherwise silent car. Thoughts of the beautiful day, the black lab waiting at home, the broken steps that must be fixed, and tomorrow were all competing with the reaching strains of the music.

Suddenly an image appeared in the lights of the car. Swerving and with great force the car struck a tree that so beautifully guided the way. The door flew open and the cold night air quickly flowed in. The adagio reached its height only to fall into the depth of a sleep never to wake again.

CHAPTER ONE

♥

The old stone mansion, darkened by age, looked elegant that warm August evening. It sat among the towering oaks and late summer flower gardens of reds, yellows and soft purples. Its massive pillars guarded the welcoming doors. The receptive warmth of the southern style structure served well in this mid–western state.

The estate had been bequeathed to the city by John Bellamy for cultural events such as art shows and photo exhibits. A vast collection of original photos, film and art sat in their archives. Inside, the ballroom had been elegantly decorated for the photography clubs special event of the year. The evening sun reflected through the long red–and–blue stained glass windows and glimmered softly on the large crystal chandelier. Original paintings and antique furniture were arranged in small vignettes around the edge of the ballroom. Silver candlesticks and vases adorned the ornately carved mantle and the other small tables.

Christina was admiring the room from several angles. She had been responsible for the additional decorations for the evening event. Small tables had been added for members and their guests. The tables were covered with skirts of rainbow colors and arranged in an arch around the center of the ballroom. On each table was a small vase of fresh colorful flowers. The guest table too had a colorful skirt and a larger bouquet. The pinks, yellows and blue of the mixed flowers added richness to the décor. Their fragrance played lightly around the room. The combination of old beauty and the new decorations made the overall appearance elegant and welcoming.

"Christina my dear," Mrs. Craig interrupting her observations, "Your decorating is so perfect for the evening. It is such a delight to have you in the club. We need more young people like you. You should have joined sooner."

"Thank you, I enjoyed the decorating. It's great to be a part of the group."

As Mrs. Craig moved on to greet arriving guests, she left Christina with a feeling of self–assurance and satisfaction that her decorating efforts were successful. Christina had worked hard to give the ballroom an elegant appearance for the guest of honor.

♥

Daniel Halloran was that special guest.

His presence was quite an honor. Although his residence was in the big city, north of here, a busy schedule kept him mostly away on assignments. The club had wanted to honor him at their special summer gathering and he too was honored to be asked. The planning committee for the evening had attended to all the details. Everything appeared to be in order as the club members and invited guests were beginning to arrive.

Christina walked and chatted among the arriving guests. She knew many of them since childhood because her family had always lived in the area.

She caught sight of Mr. Rheinbach, her high school art teacher, now retired. She made her way to him.

"Mr. Rheinbach how are you?"

"Christina, what a delight. I guess the last time I saw you was when I visited school a while ago. And how have you been?"

"We've been very good. Thank you."

"Are you a guest or did you join the club?"

"I joined last year. Photography has always been a challenge and something new to learn and I also help with the club at school."

"I see your father at the business luncheon occasionally. Retirement has been good for him, for both of us. Moreover, he told me about your showing at the Nature Gallery. That is really great."

"Yes, late winter sometime. He is helping me choose. They want about ten. It is probably going to be mostly landscapes. I have more of them than any other."

"That would be an excellent choice. You are very good at developing a scene and making it come to life. You should have been an art teacher."

"No. I feel limited in that field. I could never draw faces or the body. And I just don't like using water color. I am very happy teaching literature."

"Your mother was proud that you made that choice. This young man that is here tonight is quite a talented photographer. The pictures in his books are beautiful and the writing is also very descriptive. Mr. Sanborn, who invited me, tells me that he asked his speaking fee go to a local children's charity."

Christina thought that was very nice of him.

"My dear it is so nice seeing you and have a good evening. And let me know when your show opens."

"You're on my invitation list. You were certainly an inspiration for me."

Christina considered painting a hobby, but she had developed her natural talent all through high school and college. She found it relaxing and an escape from the pressures of everyday life.

Although she only knew the guest of honor from news clipping and stories from others, she had looked forward to this event and was sure it would be very interesting to hear him speak.

Suddenly there was an extra murmur from the welcoming committee near the door. Dan had arrived. Just then his tall, large, handsome man came through the door. He presented a most charming smile. In his dark blue summer attire, his appearance was flawless.

His radiant mannerisms and exciting words opened the conversation with ease. He greeted each one as if they were special.

"I feel so honored to be here," he told Mr. Anderson. "It feels good because this area was home for a while," he added further with definite expression. "The folks here have been so kind through the years. You have always written nice articles and now a gracious welcome for me," he offered another. He continued to exchange other words of welcome with those who were receiving him. His warmth and charm radiated as he moved among the group. It was obvious he was happy to be at this event in his honor.

Christina stood aside talking with others. She was not one of the initial receptionists, but her presence did not go unnoticed for long. Glancing ahead Dan caught sight of her.

Her red dress was perfect against the blue–stained glass window. Although a little captivated by her beauty, his first thought was, she would be perfect to photograph. With the combination of blue, red and a lovely lady, that would make a perfect picture. He stared at her. Who is this beautiful lady?

Soon she became aware that he was staring and the attention found her unguarded. She offered one of her broad captivating smiles. Smiling back was a natural for him.

After a few more handshakes and words of welcome Dan discreetly edged his way toward this lovely lady in the red dress. Christina noticed that he was moving her way.

"I'm Dan Halloran, I don't believe I know you," he stated and extended his hand. That warm captivating smile again came over Christina as she introduced herself.

"I'm Christina Zeller," and she also offered her hand.

Dan could feel that it was warm and firm. He gazed intently into her sparkling soft brown eyes. He noticed her medium brown hair that fell below her shoulders and then gave a twist. He noticed her perfectly proportioned face that wore a soft summer tan. She broke his enchanting thoughts as she pulled away her hand.

He could not believe how this young woman had attracted him. He had been exposed to many areas of the world and photographed many women, but right here in his old home town he was utterly enchanted by this lovely lady, which he had just seen for the first time in his life, so he thought. He was mesmerized by her presence. He could not believe how he felt. He glanced casually to see if her hand adorned a ring. It did not.

As the other people moved around the ballroom, Dan continued to talk to Christina. "I'm here to talk about my latest book."

"And I am here to hear about it," she replied.

"Can I assume that you are part of the group and then you must live in the area?"

"Yes, we have a farm south of here," she replied.

That *we* sounded loud to Dan and he wondered, who *we* are?

"Cows?" he asked with a smile.

"No," she responded warmly and with a sensuous laugh. "My father leases the farm land and the stables out. We just have the house and a small bit of land to look after."

An inward sigh of relief came over Dan. I don't believe she is married, he thought, but there is always a chance she has a special friend. Not wearing a ring was not always telling. I'll take my chance and get to know her better.

He changed the subject. "This seems to be an interesting group of people. Their interest in photography overwhelms me," he said as he glanced over the crowd. "I understand they do many things to promote art and how it can be used. Someone told me some of the people have taken tours to photograph different parts of the country, so the photos can be used for educational materials."

"Yes, their interest and the things they provide are certainly very useful and I hear they have lots of fun too."

"What is your interest in the club?" he inquired.

Christina replied hesitantly, "I have only been meeting with the group since last winter. Photography is mainly a serious hobby for me. Although I take pictures with particular themes and I have my students use them for creative writing. They seem to enjoy doing that and I also help with the photography club at school."

He listened with interest and questioned, "You're a teacher?"

"Yes. I'm in the English department at Brigham High, I also graduated from there."

"I once met guys from Brigham, but I attended Saint Francis up north. We played your school in sports and I was down here once with our debate club. We lived here only one summer and I didn't have time to get to know anyone, although I made my way around the city by myself and found some really interesting things. Bellamy House being one of them. Then we moved further north. It was more centralized for my dad."

She again nodded with a smile and before she could answer he continued talking about the school.

"You attended Brigham and now you teach there?"

"I do."

"How does it feel to be in this situation, once a student, now a teacher in the same school?"

"There are lots of memories, but my being in a different position, it has its own identity. A few of the teachers are still there and that is a definite link with the past."

"Where did you say your farm was?" Dan quizzed her.

"South, off Lake Road."

Just as they were about to enjoy more conversation, Mr. Baker interrupted, "Dan, if you would join the others at the guest table, our program can get under way."

Dan quickly said to Christina, "We can continue this conversation later." And he went with Mr. Baker.

♥

As the guest of honor and officers were seated, the other guests took their places at the colorful decorated tables. The chairman made various announcements and other orders were presented. Dan needed no introduction, but he was presented to the group by Mr. Baker.

"Daniel Halloran lived in our area for a short time some years ago, but we consider him one of our own. His accomplishments as a photographer are many for his young age of thirty. He had been involved with documentaries, television commercials, and special assignments throughout the world. He has also received the coveted prize in photography for his photo–essay book about the 1967 riots. It tells the story of the people who were left in the wake of the tragedy that had otherwise been forgotten. He is here this evening to talk about his latest achievement a photo–essay book about children. He will be discussing the events that helped bring this book together and of course he will be autographing."

The members of the club and other invited guests gave Dan a warm welcome as he stood tall behind the lectern. The last ray of the setting sun that played carefully throughout the ballroom, making his black hair glisten. His actions and movements were smooth and polished. He stood for a moment just smiling at the group.

"I'm so glad to be among home folks. To see old friends again and sure to make new ones."

He beamed as he began to speak about his newly published book. His every word seemed to flow with ease.

"Unusual that the theme should be children, because photographing children has not been a major part of my business. This started as a casual approach and has evolved over several years. It didn't start out to be a book, but as my collections of images became larger the idea took shape. My publisher liked it so it came to be and was launched several months ago in Chicago, where I have a residence. In my travels as a photographer, I seemed to encounter children and as photographers do, I took pictures. One day I started putting them in order and I found a continuity in their actions, where race and country has no preference. A simple piece of paper that holds their image reveals so much. It seems to say the same for children all over the world. These photos reveal their emotions such as loneliness, bewilderment, fear, and their need for love and attention as well as happiness. Also, innocently they reveal the habits that are unique to their small world. Some are from Kenya, some from Vietnam, and others from here in the United States. But as one views the photos it is hard to tell which country they are from. What a story these photos tell about young people from all over the world."

Dan continued to discuss his experience. "Some were pure happiness and today I think about what I saw and have to laugh. Others were very sad and those thoughts give me pause. I have only a second of time on paper but I noted in my journal what the day was like, the culture, was this an area of poverty or affluence—and I had to make my notes as accurately as possible—affluence in one particular culture might appear poverty in another. I also noted was it raining or hot, what kind of sound were in the environment, were there other people nearby, were we inside or outside, very basic things. A photo stimulates our imagination and accurate words will enhance it. I try to be very accurate with the entire atmosphere and leave my own feelings as a footnote in my journal. Overall it was a great experience and I'm glad I took advantage of it."

While he talked his eyes quickly scanned the group. He was looking for Christina. Her red dress should be easy to find, he thought. Again he scanned the crowd. He did not see her. He hoped she had not slipped out of his life as quickly as she had come in. Where had she gone?

His discussion came to an end with his words about the dedication. "Hopefully this collection can be a memorial to these and all children, especially to those who have never had the opportunity to become adults. As you know, I aptly dedicated this book to Melissa Halloran, my young sister, who was very dear to me. Even after all these years her memory is yet very strong. So this is for her."

There was a silence as Dan paused and looked over the group one more time. Christina was there. His eyes locked in her direction. Happily he said, "And I will autograph the books for anyone that so requests, and with great delight I thank you for the opportunity to be here with you this evening."

Mr. Baker replaced Dan at the lectern. "Thank you Dan, for sharing the joys of your book with us. We're all honored that you would take time from your busy schedule to be with us this evening. Let's extend a warm hand to him and hope he will often share his creative abilities with us. Thank you again, Dan."

Mr. Baker led the group in giving him an extended applause.

"If you have not had the opportunity to get a copy of Dan's books, they are both in the foyer, Mrs. Anderson will be there. Dan's earlier book contains beautiful photos and a vivid description of a slice of American history as it happened.

History in the making and he has done it so beautifully. We should have more of these and recommended for your collection. Everyone is invited to the garden room for champagne and hors d'oeuvre while Dan autographs his books here in the ballroom," was Mr. Baker last announcement.

Some of the guests went for champagne, some joined in conversation, while others waited for Dan. He seated himself at the Queen Anne writing desk and quickly occupied himself in autographing and in conversation with different individuals. All the while Dan was looking for Christina. He did not want her to get away before he could become better acquainted.

Christina wanted to ask for his personal touch to be added to her book. She soon made her way to Dan with it in hand. He smiled with pleasure as he took it and wrote:

> *To Christina,*
> *May I take you to dinner tomorrow evening?*
> *Daniel*

He handed the book to her open so she was sure to note his request.

Dan felt relaxed that he had made a definite contact before she could get away. Now it is up to her.

Christina casually glanced at her book to see what message Dan had scrawled. She was so surprised at his offer that she just smiled and looked around to see if anyone had read the note. She smiled at him briefly as she moved quickly away, other people were waiting. Does he really want to take me to dinner? She asked herself as she moved quickly among the guests. She joined in conversation with Mrs. Williams, although she hardly heard what they were talking about. Many questions were racing through her mind. Why is he asking me? Surely he knows many beautiful models. He probably has a woman in every port, as they say. And how clever writing in my book.

But despite her thoughts she was excited to think Dan had notice her and invite her to have dinner with him. How can I tell him that I would be delighted to join him? He seemed to be constantly occupied with other guests.

He talked and laughed with the guests, but often he would look around the room. His search would stop when his eyes fell upon Christina. He enjoyed talking about his book and other things, but at this time it seemed obvious that he wanted, very much, to talk to her. Several times she had left the ballroom and each time he feared she could be leaving. She can't leave now, he thought. How would I get in touch with her? These and other thoughts were loud in his mind. He had the urge to just get up from this desk and follow her and get to know her better, but he remained composed, smiled and signed his name. He knew she had read what he had written and he felt somehow she had to answer.

After what seemed like hours, Dan had finished autographing the books. He noticed Christina was still there and was casually chatting with two of the younger guests. Without hesitation he made his way in her direction. All talk stopped and they turned their attention to Dan.

"Did you have a glass of champagne?"

"No, I haven't, I've been signing my name, and no one even offered to bring me one," he said playfully.

"Well, let's correct that right now."

"But first, Dan this is Zack and James from the photography club. They both have done some very interesting work and last year they worked together on posters for several of the school's events."

"Very interesting and I would like to see some of your work and get a different perspective."

Christina smiled. "How about that glass of champagne?"

They excused themselves from the young people and made their way to the garden room.

Dan poured two glasses of champagne and handed her one, "To a great evening."

Dan relaxed because he felt he had overcome the first step to getting to know her. I've captured her attention, and if she has no attachments, I'll be pleased.

As they sipped their champagne they continued their conversation. "This evening has been one of the nicest receptions that I have had in honor of my book. There were several others, but this one obviously has many personal touches. That made it special. Were you one of the people responsible for getting this evening together?"

"In a small way. I planned the decorations and the color scheme. Several of my students helped to get things in order. There were two others, but they had to leave."

She laughed, "That was part of the agreement. If they helped, they could attend. They were very excited to hear you speak about your work. One of the young men is especially interested in a career in journalism."

"Also I want to tell you that I think your book is very beautiful. For several days I have been looking at it and each time I see more. It's a great addition to my collection." She clutched it tightly.

"Also I have your other book and had I thought I would have brought it to be autographed."

"That can be arranged," he quickly responded.

Christina looked around, noticing that many of the guests had left. "I believe it is time for all of us to be leaving. I have a box that I must put in my car."

Quickly Dan picked up on the conversation. "If it is a large box then you need me to help you."

The words quickly brought a deep smile. "If you would like, but it is in the back of the house," she said as she pointed the way.

They strolled through several rooms on their way to the back.

"This is a beautiful house and so many beautiful antiques and paintings. My visit was a long time ago," Dan said.

"I believe most were here when Mr. Bellamy lived here."

"The house and then the archives. This certainly is a treasure for the city."

She was wondering if he would mention dinner again as they continued through the long hall to the back.

"This is it, not too big," she said as she pointed to the box of things that must be taken home. "My car isn't too far."

"Good night all!" they called to the few people still there as she and Dan exited through the back way.

"It has been rather warm here this summer," he said as they walked to her car. He wanted to say something more dynamic but felt lost for words. He had been excited all evening by just looking at her, but there appeared to be more to her than her beauty. He could hardly believe his feelings and what a surprise.

"Too much hot weather without rain is certainly bad for crops. Some have really suffered."

"But you don't farm?"

"It's all farmed by others, but we see the effects. My father and I, and of course the dogs, live in the big house. My mother passed a few years ago and my brothers are married.

He listened tentatively and responded with an "Oh," that seemed to come from deep thoughts.

As they reached her car she said, "You can put it in the back." Dan placed the box in the car and she quickly closed the door.

"Could we have that dinner tomorrow evening? That is if you don't have other plans. Or if there is another person in your life, I don't wish to intrude." He hated to say that but felt strongly he must get it out and over with.

She smiled warmly, "Dinner would be very nice." Dinner and that will be all. Then he'll be back to his worldly events, whatever they are and I'll be back to mine.

"Great. I will call for you and how do I get to your farm?"

"The main highway south, exit Lake Road, to Pitcher, a right and then not far is a large red mail box. On the post is our landmark, ZELLER FARMS and STABLES. That's us. Turn in the drive and you are there. It's a big old stone house."

"Sounds easy enough. How about six o'clock and if you approve we'll drive out to the Carriage House." She tried not to show excitement as she gave her approval.

He took her hand and kissed her lightly on the cheek, "Until tomorrow."

She too, had been attracted to this near stranger. The first sight of him had brought an inner pleasure that had lasted throughout the evening. His words and gestures had brought contentment as she watched him carefully. It was like a great joy had entered her life. She was observing a new feeling in herself. It was new and different and so very pleasing, but would it all be in vain.

♥

Christina got into her little red car and started off into the dark night. As she drove, many thoughts started and she told herself not to get excited over a simple dinner engagement. Dan is a man from the world I do not know. High fashion photographer, widely traveled, he moves among the elite as their guest and artist. He probably had many romances and I do not want to be another. He will be gone in a few days. I probably will not see him for a long time or perhaps never again. Anyway, I do not feel ready to get involved in another romance. The scar in my heart has not healed.

She turned in the long drive to her home and saw the tiny light gradually get larger. It was the light that was always on, always waiting. As she stopped her car her dogs, Daisy a black standard poodle and Henry a black lab, greeted her in silence. They never barked at her or her father, only strangers. She stopped for a moment and gave them assurance and affection. They followed her into the house for they knew it was time to go to bed.

Christina found that her father had retired. After a few moments of doing nothing in the kitchen she decided to go to her bedroom and read. As she undressed she thought of Dan. How would his lips feel on mine? His body was big and towering. How would it feel to be in his arms? It had been a long time since she had allowed anyone near her. It would almost be a new experience.

Christina turned out the light, opened her drapes and slipped into bed. She lay quietly and listened to the sounds of night. The silent wind moved the giant oaks to gently touch the house. Through the window she could see the night clouds and the moon in the darkened sky. The insects were in full chorus and in the distance a quiet hoot of an owl could be heard. It was a typical warm, summer night with the usual sights and sounds.

She kept seeing Dan's handsome face in the night. She kept hearing his gentle, but confident voice. She remembered how his dark eyes often came to rest upon her. She imagined his arms around her and she easily fell asleep.

CHAPTER TWO

♥

The morning air touched lightly on Christina's face. The early sun streamed calmly into her bedroom. She sat up and stretched vigorously. She went quickly into the shower for a fresh start.

Waking was beautiful today. Her first thought was of Dan. She remembered several commentaries in the newspapers over the years. Only his accomplishments had been reviewed but nothing of his personal life—and she had not given these articles much attention. Was he really the gentle giant he appeared to be? Or was he like those ruthless photographers, always harassing celebrities? She hoped he had not been guilty of such incidents.

It appeared he did not need to resort to these actions to gain publicity. He seemed too sophisticated and intelligent for these actions. She did not know Dan, but from books and pictures, she knew the world in which he lived and this made her a bit skeptical. Meeting him had been interesting. Having dinner with him would be exciting and was certainly an added surprise to her life, but then back to the usual.

She heard her father call, "Chris, are you all right? Are you awake honey?"

She opened her bedroom door and called, "I'll be down very soon Papa."

In the kitchen she fixed her coffee and sat quietly at the table with her father. A smile crossed her face.

"Papa, do you remember Dan Halloran who spoke at Bellamy House last night?" she asked.

"Yes—that young man was here once. I believe your brother Bill brought him here. They drove out with Mr. Redman one Saturday afternoon. I don't remember why."

Christina was very surprised! "Really, I don't remember that! When was that?"

"When the boys were in high school."

"A while ago. Wonder if he remembers? I won't mention it and see if he does. I don't."

Her four brothers had many friends that had come and gone during high school and being a few years younger she didn't give them much attention.

"He asked me to have dinner with him this evening. He wrote the message in his book that he was autographing for me. But then he asked me later if I had no plans and he also asked if there was anyone special in my life that he didn't wish to intrude."

"Really? How nice," her father replied slowly.

"I feel as excited as a school girl," she responded.

"Chris, don't be too hasty with your feelings." He paused. "You should be dating, but I don't want to see you hurt again."

"Papa, I know, I don't want to be hurt either." She paused and gave a nostalgic glance into the bright morning sky. "It's rather impossible. I could . . . " Her words trailed off into the silence as she gazed into the blue beyond. Searching. Her life had once been as bright as the sky, but darkened by someone gone forever. She had cautioned herself never to be hurt again. The next few moments were only moments, but it seemed like hours as her thoughts of Brian lived over and over.

Her father interrupted her silence. "He has been all over the world. Takes pictures of models. He doesn't know what settling down means or he probably would have been married by now. How long is he going to be here?"

"I'm not sure," she hesitated. "He didn't say. Anyway, Papa, it's only dinner! Who's talking about settling down?" she briskly replied and tried to hide her excitement.

"His folks lived somewhere north of the city. I remember them. They moved years ago. Where is he staying?"

"He didn't say," she casually replied. She felt a bit disillusioned after hearing those words from her father, but he was probably right, she thought.

"You're right Papa, our life styles are worlds apart. I'm only a school teacher and he is a well–known photographer."

She said no more to her papa but her thought continued. A professional photographer cannot compare to my quiet life teaching Shakespeare and Steinbeck to young people. They're probably many women in his life. He's so handsome. Oh, why am I thinking all of these unnecessary thought? This will be only one dinner engagement.

"Honey, I am going to drive to Benton's this morning and check about the new horses that arrived last week."

"Okay, I have things to do around here. I also have a school project that I have to finish. It won't be long till it starts again. When are you taking the dogs for their bath?"

"I made arrangements for Wednesday," he added as he was about to leave.

♥

It was a long time before Christina had to get ready for her evening with Dan. She did a few things around the house and laid out her unfinished school project on the dining table and was about to begin working when the phone rang.

"Hello."

"Christina," a big voice asked.

"Yes."

"This is Dan Halloran. We have dinner plans for this evening."

In an instant Christina thought of many things, he's calling to cancel. At least he called rather than just not show up!

"I was going to stay in my hotel room and do some planning but I must have left my notebook in the city. So I noticed a poster about the photo exhibit called "The Thirty's Authors" at the gallery. I know it is short notice, but if you do not have plans, I would like for you to join me, since we both have interest in the subject, I believe we could enjoy the show together. I won't keep you long, a couple hours."

Dan waited and there seemed to be a long silence, but finally Christina said slowly. "No I don't have any plans. I heard it's a real good show. It's an interesting theme."

"Then you'll join me," he sounded happy about her decision. "Should I come out for you?"

"It will save some time, why don't I drive in and meet you at the gallery. There is a parking lot in the back and a back entrance. How about meeting there?"

"At the back entrance it is. Would eleven–thirty be too soon?"

"That would be okay," she responded.

"See you then," and they ended their conversation.

Christina cleared her work from the table and went to change into something appropriate for the gallery. She wrote a note to her father telling him that Dan had called and invited her to go to the gallery and she would be home around three o'clock.

A twenty–minute drive would take her into the city and another five to the gallery. She arrived promptly at eleven–thirty and found Dan waiting in the lounge by the back entrance. He came to meet her. "I'm so glad you could come and we could enjoy the show together, even on such short notice," he said almost in words of apology.

"It is a nice surprise," she added. "I've wanted to come in and see it but just kept putting it off."

"I have our tickets, and we're ready to begin, but there is a little café upstairs, would you like to get a sandwich first. It is a long time until our dinner," he asked.

"It is a while, sounds good," she answered happily.

As they enjoyed their sandwich the conversation flowed freely.

Dan asked, "How long have you been teaching?"

"Two years. Start the third next month. I came home after graduate school and was lucky to get the position."

"I'm sure you deserved it, but maybe a little luck that there was an opening."

"Have you always been a photographer?"

"Always. I have a tough time getting here, but I made it. I decided late in college, so I had to spend an extra year getting the requirements. I've never been sorry that I had all those extra classes. I feel that it enriched me."

"What was your first choice?"

"I wanted to be a history teacher in college and write . . . I just loved the subject. Any period of time. I still read old and new books, when I have the time."

"What made you change?"

"My roommate didn't want to go to this lecture alone and finally consenting, it changed my life. It was a lecture by a photographer and he had photos of various subjects and he explained how he created them. He discussed themes, construction, night, day. And that was it for me. I thought I could incorporate history and everything else in a career of photography. And that I've tried."

"That's amazing and it happened overnight."

"More like over an hour."

"Your books certainly reflect history. Your first one especially. And your writing is very descriptive."

"Thank you. How about taking in the show downstairs?"

He took her hand as they walked into the room.

"Oh my, this is great," Dan said as he glanced around. "Where was this collection originally?"

"I believe I read in a review when it opened that most are from Bellamy House."

"To go through those archives would be a photographer's dream. Probably could spend a lifetime doing that."

"Steinbeck."

Dan read aloud. "A San Francisco newspaper requested Steinbeck go to southern California and write articles about the migrant workers. These are some of the photos he took while there."

"Look Chris at these sad pictures. All they own is tied on that old car. Here's another in a cart. No smiles. There wasn't anything to smile about. Just despair. And they are going to a place almost as bad as they're leaving."

Chris added, "*Grapes of Wrath* came out of this. As telling as words are, your profession captures the emotions and a legacy in just one click, poverty, loneliness, helplessness."

"That is why I love my profession and hopefully I can do it justice with my creativity and imagination," he responded.

She looked at him and caught his eyes and said, "You have."

"Thank you," he said as he kissed her lightly on the cheek.

Oh my Christina thought, I hope he didn't notice what I felt.

"Now we have Faulkner," Dan said as they moved on still holding her hand. "He looks like a lawyer. And his typewriter."

"He had a wide variety of characters in his work, but most were southern."

"I'm going to ask who's your favorite," he said as he gazed into her soft brown eyes.

"Don't do that, I can't answer," she smiled contentedly receiving his gaze.

Chris felt that look and it translated, for her, into something warm and wonderful. I'm reading too much she thought.

"F. Scott Fitzgerald, a guy that puzzles me. How could he write so much while drinking as much as they say," was Dan's comment. "Here are several with Zelda. His eyes are really captured in this one."

"He did most of his work in the twenties, but some of his more well–known are from the thirties," Chris added.

"Here's Sinclair Lewis looking pensive. They took this picture straight on, but you see that his thoughts are elsewhere."

Dan turned to Chris. "Are you enjoying this and are you listening to the background music?"

"Oh yes, I'm glad you ask me to join you," she said with delight in her voice. "And yes I hear the music. The art forms complement each other so very much."

"Now we have Hemingway, a local. He was born in Oak Park," Dan said.

"Such a macho person but his work is so from the heart."

"Yeah, he was everywhere and did everything. World War One, Spanish Civil, D–Day, Liberation of Paris, four wives. What a guy," and he laughed.

"Here's Thomas Wolfe. We're not done, but I believe I can say he is my favorite in this group," she said.

"Why is that?"

"It's personal. I like his style, you can identify with his characters. The way he writes."

"Finally we have two ladies. Willa Cather and Pearl Buck." They paused to read and look at the pictures and then walked on.

"I like Pearl Buck's work a lot. Her work is so varied. East and West. Many themes," Chris said.

"And they didn't forget James Hilton. *Lost Horizon,* I like a lot."

As they looked at the last group Dan glanced at his watch. "Timed just right, two hours. I don't want you to have to rush to get home for that date with that big guy," he smiled.

"I won't have to rush, but I am looking forward to tonight," she happily answered back. "I enjoyed this very much and I'm glad you thought of me."

Looking her way with closed eyes and a smile, he shook his head yes and thought, not hard at all.

They both had enjoyed the show, but they also secretly watched each other. It was their own way of getting to know each other. Expression, gestures, slight shake of the head and more, it had told much.

"Tonight we'll have a real date," he smiled. It was a happy smile, a contented smile, a smile for Christina.

He walked with her to her car and said, "I'm sure I can find your house okay, not too many turns and your instructions last evening seemed good." With that he kissed her lightly on the cheek and they parted, she to her home and Dan to the hotel.

♥

She arrived home and papa's car was there so he must be around somewhere, she thought. She went straight to her room to relax before getting ready for the evening.

After relaxing for about twenty minutes she went to look for her father. She found him in the back garage rearranging and making space for another car.

They would need the space at Christmas when the family would all be home.

She told him of her day with Dan and spoke briefly about the exhibit. "And we're still going to have dinner tonight. He said it would be a real date," she said as she smiled.

With that she left her father and went to her bedroom to get ready for the evening. It was an exceptionally quiet time of the day. A warm shower soothed her tanned body. A Chopin Etude could be heard on the radio from her bedroom. Christina was not giving much thought to anything. She was just basking in the sensual feelings of the moment. She briskly toweled herself dry to generate some vitality to her relaxed body.

She chose her powder blue dress for this special evening. Her selection was distinctly revealing in a tasteful and unassuming way. It was her favorite and she felt comfortable wearing it. The brush went through her soft brown hair many times. Earrings. A touch of pink on her cheeks added to the glow of soft radiance. A faint touch of summer fragrance made everything complete. She stared at herself in the mirror, afraid to be joyful.

Suddenly she was very conscious of her overall appearance. She had never been totally aware of her beauty. Her taste in clothes, although colorful, had always been chosen from the less extravagant designers. She had never needed glittering jewelry or wrenching strength of heavy make–up to complete herself. She had always preferred simplicity. Knowing Dan, as a visual artist, would be aware of every small facet of her body and clothes, she hoped he would find her attractive.

♥

She was ready and waiting patiently, for it was a bit past the time Dan said he would arrive. As she watched from the big window at the front of her home, she saw a car in the distance. It drove slowly through the oak lined drive to the house. It could only be Dan. She watched him as he slowly got out of his dark blue car. The dogs barked as they rushed to greet him. He didn't seem to mind. He first offered his free hand to Daisy and then to Henry. A pat on the head and a rub behind the ears seemed to please them. He then looked with admiration at the large stone farmhouse and the surrounding area.

The dogs ran beside him as he made his way up the walk and to the front door. Christina was watching all. He was as handsome and stylish as he had been in the afternoon and the evening before. She opened the door to greet him.

"Even though the time has been short, it is good to see you again dear Christina. I hope I'm not too late, I made a wrong turn," he stated.

She responded casually. "Wrong turn, that happens."

His eyes caught the beauty of her slender body that not even a dress could hide. The neckline revealed that her breasts were small. The skirt hung loosely over her narrow but rounded hips. He embraced her with his dark and passionate eyes. Without further greetings, he handed her the deep red rosebud that he clutched in his hand and said, "A lovely rose for a lovely lady."

"Oh, thank you, it's so thoughtful of you." The smile she returned said much to his eyes.

"You look lovely. Blue is my favorite color," he said as he slightly lifted his eyes and a hint of a smile arched his mouth.

"Thank you. Come and meet my Papa. He remembers you." Dan followed Chris into the library. Papa Zeller was behind the newspaper.

"Papa, this is Dan."

"Oh yes," he said as he dropped the paper and rose to accept Dan's extended hand in renewed acquaintance. "Of course I remember Dan. You were here once, what seems like years ago."

Yes!" Dan exclaimed. "I realized as I was coming up the drive. Your brother Bill? and you came out Mr. Zeller."

"Call me John."

Still in amazement he turned to her to be corrected. She shook her head yes. "I came out here with him and several other guys to get something, as I recall. When I turned in the driveway something was so familiar. It's all coming back to me now. I remember the long drive and this beautiful house. And one other thing that comes to me, a little girl running with two German shepherds. Was that you?" He was so delighted to remember!

She too was excited that he had been at their home and also remembered. To her it made him a home folk, not just a world traveled photographer.

"It must have been me. I've always been here and we had two German shepherds, Chloe and Sable," she acknowledged.

The excitement quieted and Dan turned to Chris and said, "Should we treat ourselves to that dinner at the Carriage House?"

"Yes, but first come with me while I put this beautiful rose in a vase."

Dan said good night to Papa Zeller and followed her. She chose a crystal bud vase and placed it on the dining room table.

"It's so perfect. I'll take it to my room later," she said as she touched it lightly.

"I called today and they have reservations for us at seven–thirty. If I remember it will be timed just right," he said as he glanced at his watch.

Outside he took her hand as they walked to his big blue car. It was a nice gesture that made her feel warm. Dan too felt the same way.

♥

The drive to the Carriage House was filled with more conversation about getting to know each other. Christina began the casual conversation. "Tell me about some of the things you've done, your photo projects."

"I have had many types of assignments."

"That's more interesting," she interjected.

"Interesting, well yes, but hard. For two years I worked for *World Scene Magazine* and yes interesting but not quite fulfilling for me. They sent us out in twos and we were all over, Japan for a few days, then India the next few, then on to Alaska. Anywhere there was trouble or something exciting. But we only got a small flavoring. The journalist did the reporting for the moment then someone else back at the office would go in depth."

"You were traveling and seeing the world."

"But the traveling, well it wasn't traveling, it was just moving around fast and it was killing me. I didn't have a social life. I wasn't able to eat properly or sleep properly. When my contract was up I did not renew. But I became known and that helped my career along," and he paused.

"You must have many photos from that time."

"Many, and my journal is full."

"What did you do after *World?*"

"That was in 1967 and I free-lanced. There had been race riots in many U.S. cities earlier that year, so I went back into the areas to look for human interest stories and to photograph the effects. I had to gain the confidence of the people and they let me photograph them and tell their story. It wasn't hard at all. Most of them were desperate to be heard. I only reported the effects not the why, everyone knew the why."

"Were you ever afraid or in danger?"

"Several times, I began to wonder if I should be there. But I told their story, took pictures in the day and wrote at night and that was my first book. It won me the coveted prize and my career really took off. I was so grateful. It was luck and being at the right place at the right time."

"Then you were able to accept what you wanted, not what you had to. Which is certainly much nicer."

"Yes, I went to work for the agency that I now work for. And I do still photography which I like best because I can be more creative. The agency provides work for many magazines, books, I could go on."

"I'd love to see . . . all of it."

"Most are at moms but I have some where I live in the big city."

"You work all hours and all days."

"I do. They keep me very busy. They rarely consult me, Kate the lady that is assigned to me, knows exactly what I like and don't like. I have a great relationship with her and the agency. You'll meet her. She is in her forties, has a professor husband and three teen–age daughters. She knows the business. There is a lot of work. Assignments vary with the type of work and the length of time required."

"Then people request you personally for their work?"

"Yes, as you get to be more known in the field. My agency is a little more selective. Putting it that way is certainly overstating. There are a lot of forgotten efforts, disappointments to get to this place. I've made it in the sense that I'm fully employed. There are very good photographers that struggle all their lives and eventually resort to work out of their chosen profession. Some of making it is luck, but there is a tremendous amount of hard work and sometimes doubt to go along."

"What are you working on now?"

"Several things, several things for the centennial. We're finishing a booklet for the hospital. The agency has a huge warehouse, which is our studio, with lots of props and things to work with. We do a lot of work there. We're starting a book for the symphony, interviews, rehearsals. That's going to be a lot of fun and good listening."

"Do you do ads for magazines?"

"Oh yes, many."

"Do you write text?"

"Many times a writer will be on set and we'll work together. You exchange ideas and creative thoughts. Then again they will wait until they see all the pictures."

Dan switched the conversation abruptly. "Enough about me. Do you like being a teacher?"

"Oh yes, I love it. I have never been disappointed that

I chose teaching as my career."

"It's truly a delight to find someone happy with their work. I'm sure you have noticed, I am ecstatic about what I do. "And of course you have a Master's Degree, which is why you're teach in high school."

"Yes, Papa insisted all of us go to graduate school and we all did. It wasn't hard he paid for it. We were fortunate that we didn't have to work while in school. The boys all worked during the summer. Papa always got them jobs somewhere."

"Who are the boys other than Bill?"

"I have four brothers, John, Bill, Jim and Dave."

"I believed you mentioned that your mother had passed."

"Yes. Mother passed when I first went to college."

"I'm sorry. That is so unfortunate that she was taken so early. An excellent part of your life together was just beginning." And he paused. "So you and your father and those dogs live there by yourself."

"We do."

As they exchanged words and laughs it was almost like they had known each other for years. They were very relaxed and comfortable with each other. The drive passed quickly as they continued to share experiences and answer questions about themselves.

♥

The country inn was a favorite dining place for the surrounding area. Dan parked the car and they walked through the tree–lined path to the inn.

Inside the host led them to their table. The low beamed ceiling and the quaint remnants of yesteryear offered a feeling of intimacy. The many green plants added freshness to the dining room. Soft music created a mood of togetherness. Their table was in the far corner as Christina had hoped. The host said, "It's a pleasure to have you and the lady as our guests, Mr. Halloran." Dan thanked him and they were seated.

The dining room was dim and the candles flickered peacefully. Suddenly Dan did not seem as cheerful as he had been. He seemed to study his clasped hands as they lay on the edge of the table. Then he looked into her eyes without saying a word.

Christina felt a bit awkward but tried to continue the conversation but found it shallow and without meaning.

Papa was probably right. Was he thinking of someone else? Did he wish someone else were here? Her thoughts made her presently uncomfortable. But Christina was completely wrong in her speculation.

What Dan was in deep thought about was her. He could hardly believe it true that he had been so captivated by this beautiful woman. How could I be so lucky? Make everything what it seems. Make it all true. He was thinking all this to himself.

The waiter brought the champagne that Dan had ordered when he made reservations. After a few moments their moods slowly began to change. The champagne brought back a few thoughts of last evening.

"It was such a delightful reception. Everyone made it special."

Christina asked, "How long have you been taking pictures of children?"

He answered quickly, "Vietnam. It was one of my first assignments with *World,* before all the major upheaval. I was shooting one afternoon in a small village and from nowhere this child came running toward me. I didn't know if it was a boy or girl. It ran to me and threw its arms around my legs. I was actually afraid. Remember I was much younger then. My first thoughts were, what would I do with a child?"

"What did you do?"

"Before I could do anything an older child came and they ran off together. It happened so fast, but I was relieved. I photographed them running away from me. It's the one where the little one is running and the bigger child turns and waves."

"I remember that one. There was a sweet expression on her face. I'm sure you wonder what happened to some of the children, especially Vietnam."

"I do. So often I have thought of them. So many of the villages are destroyed. Some of the photos were taken quite a while ago and the children would have grown up and I wouldn't even recognize them. You realize how different and vast this world is when you travel from one culture to another in a matter of a few days. It can be quite an adjustment. You have to ground yourself in your own environment. You can't put yourself in the middle of a culture, you have to look in on it. That is the way I approach different areas of the world. It seemed to work for me."

"That is a wonderful approach. Do you mind if I use this concept with literature?"

"Not at all."

Changing the subject he asked, "What would you like from the menu?" They talked about all the good things listed and then Dan decided on salmon and Christina the chicken special. While waiting dinner they continued their conversation while enjoying their champagne.

"I have been doing most of the talking. I'm going to ask you some questions," he smiled.

"Your classes, English and literature?"

"Yes, this year I'll be teaching basic English. One semester of Greek classics. One in English Romantic lit. And one of poetry."

"That's a hefty schedule."

"Basic English is no problem because this will be the third year and I have many preparations already. Poetry, I also have taught for two years, but I changed the poems but use the same concept to teach. There are no tests Although I do ask them to do many written analyses of every poem and I write where they can improve and also note their good ideas. They are to keep all papers and I make a copy too. They are to study the good ideas and where they can improve, and that is their test. Then I spend one class discussing all good points and where they can improve. I work directly from their papers but never mention names This way they get a lot of coverage, not just their own. And by the end of the semester everyone always grows, some more than others. In all professions there is analyzing to be done. And I try to interject ideas from different professions, like engineering, being a lawyer, that approach. It's amazing how mentally involved they can become. They just need a little guidance. This class has proven to be very good."

"That sounds like a great course."

"It's very popular. With analyzing it can be a very personal approach. It not only familiarizes them with poetry but teaches many other concepts. When we first started thinking about doing a poetry class for high school, we all had reservations. Then I talked to the principal about some ideas that I had and he liked them so all the English teachers got together and brainstormed and came up with what seems to be working quite well. There is another class and both are always full."

"Can all the students take all the classes?" he asked.

"Maybe, for the Greek, seniors first, then it's open. Juniors Romantic, second year they can start poetry, but seniors first."

"That is encouraging, to start with good literature while they're young."

"So important, studying literature teaches so much, how to think, to analyze, as well as understanding a culture. We coordinate with the history teachers too."

"You have been at this a long time."

"Yes my mother and my brother John too, would read to me things like *Children's Shakespeare* or *Book of Garden Verses* and we would talk about what things meant."

"Your brother would read to you, how nice."

"My oldest brother, John, there is eight years difference in age and you'd think we would hardly know each other, but it is just the opposite. I'm closer to him than my other brothers, at least growing up. He was just old enough to look after me in a responsible way. When he was in high school he took me for riding lessons, ice cream. A build in baby sitter. He went to the university in the city so he was home a lot. Then he went away to graduate school and I really missed him. Now I've been talking too much."

"No, absolutely not. It's getting to know you and that is what I want most to do."

Dinner fully enjoyed, Dan requested their dessert be served on the terrace. It was high and overlooked the lake. Dan took her hand in his and looked into her soft brown eyes and said, "Let's go look at that beautiful sunset before the dessert comes."

Hand in hand they walked to the edge of the terrace. The sun had just faded into the horizon, but streaks of orange and soft pink played behind the distant trees. Rays beamed upward and slowly faded to become one with the evening sky. They both stood very still gazing into the beauty of this circumstance of nature that happens every day, but every day different. Dan turned to her, cradled her face in his hands and kissed her lightly. "I think they just brought our dessert."

While enjoying the most divine patisserie she asked, "How long are you going to be here?"

"Two more days of taking pictures, and then Thursday drive up to see mom and dad. But Wednesday morning early I have an interview at the TV studio for a local art show. It's on Sundays."

"Oh yes *Art and Book Review of the Week*, I watch it all the time. It is a nice show. That is so good."

"I had an appearance in July in the city and I believe it will be about the same. They sent me some questions that they will ask. I believe it will be aired on Sunday the fifteenth and I will be working. You can tell me all about it."

"The studio is a few blocks from the hotel and I'll walk over. Then after all of that back to the big city late Thursday. An odd schedule this week. I have to work Friday, Saturday and Sunday."

"Where are you going to take pictures?" she asked.

"Tomorrow early, I have made plans to do some research at Bellamy House archives. And then go to Lancaster Park and take all sorts of pictures of the stone bridge, the gorge. They make excellent background for all kinds of photo shoots. The next day the old gristmill, for the same reasons. And," he smiled at her, "if you have no plans, I would like very much to have you come along both days."

Christina wanted to quickly say yes, but didn't want to seem too anxious, so she slowly replied, "The next two days are free, and I can also take pictures. I can use them for creative writing for my students."

"Wonderful. We both can take advantage."

An hour had passed and darkness was coming on fast. "Shall we go? They're probably tired of us by now," he said playfully.

"Yes," her only reply, but with a smile.

♥

As they walked down the tree–lined path to the car a soft warm summer breeze surrounded them. Dan stopped, turned and took Christina in his arms, holding her close.

Surprised, she hesitated to respond. A moment passed before he kissed her lightly on the forehead. Taking her hand they walked on to the car without saying a word.

While driving to her home they again chatted about many things. She could sense Dan's was anxious about her response or lack of it. She had wanted to respond but could only think of her lost love.

Dan stopped the car in front of her home and moved over closer and put his arm around her. "Just want to sit here and be near you for a few moments," he whispered. "You don't know how much I have enjoyed being with you this evening. I feel like I have known you forever."

Christina was slightly startled and her body became tense, although she tried hard not to show her feelings. His words had touched something in her past that she did not want to think about.

Feeling something awkward Dan said, "I'll walk you to the door."

Dan quickly got out of the car and came to her aid. He took her hand and they walked briskly to the house. As they reached the door he turned quickly and took her face in his hands. He gazed through the darkness into her eyes. It seemed like forever to Christina. What did he want to say, she thought?

He kissed her lightly and she was more receptive. With this closeness she yielded softly and this gentle kiss became an embrace.

Dan gently released her and she asked, "Would you like to come in for a while."

"I would, just for a few moments." He easily replied. "I would like to take another quick look at your library. It is a beautiful room."

The dogs alone welcomed Dan and Chris home and followed them into the library. Dan walked around a few moments admiring all that made this room the most popular in the house.

"A wonderful place to spend the evening reading."

"We have all spent hours doing just that."

"I don't want to stay long. I have things to get in order for Bellamy House tomorrow. I made arrangements to use the archives at eleven o'clock. After that we'll drive out to Lancaster Park for the rest of the day. Take pictures, eat and do all sorts of nice things. Dress casual. I'll call for you at ten. How does that sound?"

"Everything sounds very good," she answered softly.

"Thank you again for a beautiful evening. Till tomorrow."

They walked back to the front door and Dan pushed her hair back and gazed lovingly into her eyes and then just said, "Good night now."

CHAPTER THREE

♥

Christina had been very busy and ten o'clock seem to come fast. Dan arrived promptly and they were off to Bellamy House. Along the way Dan told her what he was looking for.

"The Agency is gathering information and pictures for a documentary for the Centennial. They want historical representations of culture, transportation, education, rural areas. They knew I was coming out for the reception and they asked me if I would go through some archives and see what I could find. They should have some from all the surrounding states. They wanted the images to show growth over the years."

"So you're really working," Chris asked.

"Yeah," he said as he smiled at her. "It's fun work, but then again all my work is fun for me." He reached for her hand, "You being with me makes it much more than fun."

Dan continued, "Your family has lived in the area, do you have any old photos?"

"We don't have any but I think my Aunt Mary could have some. She has always been interested in family history and other histories in the area. She is the family genealogist. Papa is going down there in early September. I'll have him ask her."

♥

They reached Bellamy House and drove to the parking lot.

"This is where I said my first good night to you," Dan recalled as he reached under her hair and placed his warm hand on the back of her neck and lightly massaged. His fingertips glided smoothly back and forth. It did to Chris exactly what he wanted it to do, send ripples through her whole body. Her sexy eyes told him how much she enjoyed this moment of pleasure.

"Let's go check the archives," Dan said. "Let me get my notebook," and he reached in the back of his car.

They went in and Dan introduced himself to the receptionist, "I'm Dan Halloran and Ms. Zeller and we have an appointment with Mr. Jenkins."

"Oh yes, nice to meet you, come on in. I'll take you over

"Thank you."

"Mr. Halloran I heard your reception was real nice. My mother was there."

"It was a delightful time, a beautiful reception," he said as he glanced at Christina and gave a knowing smile. "The group was so gracious and so welcoming. Tell your mother I enjoyed it very much and thank her for me."

She led Chris and Dan into a large room with many tables and viewing paraphernalia. I believe these are the books Mr. Jenkins got out for you. Have a seat and I'll tell him that you are here."

They sat down and Christina said, "It's very cool in here."

She had on Bermuda shorts because it was very warm outside and a day in the park they would be appropriate. Dan also had on shorts.

"I agree, but it has to be temperature controlled. And I don't have a jacket to put over your shoulders," he smiled playfully and continued. "Will my arm do?"

She laughed, "No I was just saying. It feels rather refreshing."

Mr. Jenkins came in and introduced himself and Dan introduced Christina.

"Yes, these are the books I got out for you. It spans a number of years, as your agency requested. If you would like copies, just write the number of the photo and the book and give it to the receptionist and we'll get them to your agency. I'll leave you. It's very nice meeting both of you and hope you're successful."

Dan and Chris started their search and he opened his notebook to write the selections.

Chris said, "Why don't you call off the numbers and I'll write."

Dan thought that was a good idea and Chris switched sides because she is right–handed. She moved close to Dan and together they looked at the photos and discussed their relevance to the project and Chris recorded.

Dan could feel the warmth of her body even though she said that she was cold. To himself, I can hardly wait to take her in my arms, to kiss her passionately, to make love to her.

When Dan first mentioned that he would like to have her come along, she thought it might be a little boring, although she didn't say anything. But now she was enjoying the visit and found it interesting. She was also impressed by the way Dan made her a part of his research. He had introduced her, he asked her opinion and even offered a jacket although he did not have one. She thought he was so considerate, so kind and in a girly term so sweet.

They went through all of the books and decided they had chosen a good representation so they decided to go. Dan gave the list to the receptionist and asks her to please thank Mr. Jenkins and that we are very grateful for his helping us.

With that Dan and Chris walked to his car. He took her hand and pulled it to his lips and softly kissed her palm.

"We did pretty good. You saw things in the photos I didn't see. I'm glad you came with me."

♥

They were in the car and were on their way to Lancaster Park. The drive would be about forty-five minutes.

"Would you like to stop for a quick lunch?" Dan asked her.

"Not unless you do. I had a big breakfast."

"I had a big breakfast too. Eggs, toast, fruit. More than I usually eat that early. I'll treat us to an early dinner," he assured her.

As they drove they discussed what they had just seen. "There were some rather interesting images and many were taken with care and not just a quick snap," Dan offered.

"How are they going to use them?"

"I don't know, it is in the early planning stage. I just follow instructions and get the pictures."

Their first stop in the park for picture taking was at the Old Range Bridge. They walked a few feet to the creek bed. Red wild flowers were growing unattended at the base of the stone bridge. There were large and small rocks in the stream, smoothed by water over time. Weathered logs in the stream and along the bank would frame their photos. The shallow water moved in and out among the rocks and the flat sheets of limestone had formed a very tiny waterfall that crossed the entire creek. After a few pictures they both just stopped and enjoyed the view. It was a quaint vignette in this vast park.

"This is one of my favorite spots. The stone bridge and how it curves, a perfect spot for pictures."

"Many little bits of nature have created a beautiful scene. I didn't have to arrange a thing except, just take the picture."

Back in the car their next stop was at the main overlook into the gorge. Chris got out and walked to the edge.

She motioned for Dan, "Look at the river. It is just a line down there, almost empty. It's an indication of how dry it has been this summer."

"And would you look at that." Dan pointed to the other side of the gorge. "The suns angle has shadowed it so it looks like the formation is divided. What a great capture. Our timing was perfect here."

"Hurry and get that picture. In a moment this scene will change again." Chris said.

Dan and Chris made several more stops and captured the beauty of this sunny day at Lancaster Park.

Once again in the car Dan started the conversation. "It's almost five o'clock. Would you like to go down to the inn and have something to eat? We could call it a late lunch or an early dinner. Or do you have to be home to fix dinner for your father?"

"Food would be good," she replied. "We have certainly worked up an appetite. Papa always fixes his meals if I'm not there and sometimes if I am. I was in college when my mother passed and he being very conscious of eating properly, he started preparing good meals for himself."

"We passed the inn earlier, I wasn't sure if it was still there. I haven't been this way in a while. So let's check it out."

♥

The inn was a very popular stop in the park for lunch and dinner. It was an old house converted to a bed and breakfast and it was filled with antiques. Outside was beautifully groomed and the gardens were filled with colorful summer flowers and bushes. It sat at the top of one of the many hills and the upper falls was just a few steps away. This time of day was not very busy, too late for lunch and too early for dinner. Dan and Chris were quickly escorted to their table.

They ate heartily and talked happily. After the last bite of dessert, Dan suggested they go out and enjoy the falls. As they walked along the path the mist from the water lightly covered them.

"Let's get out of this shower." Dan suggested. They hurried up the path that led to the end of the garden. They relaxed on a small bench just basking in the ancient formation of the gorge and listening to the rush of the water and feeling the warm breeze as it passed by.

Dan stretched his arm across the back of the bench then after a few minutes again he reached up and massaged her neck. She moved her head sideways and closed her eyes basking in his touch.

She turned and looked at him, "You know how good that feels after such a hard day of moving around."

"No I don't but you can show me," and he smiled at her being pleased with his answer.

Chris did not know how to reply and she only smiled.

"Feeling and seeing are all part of this wonderful moments, and all the while we're listening to nature's music."

They looked at each other in a very satisfied way and then they became more serious as they discussed the beauty and the formations they had observed and photographed earlier in the day.

"The geology here is absolutely fascinating. I must do some reading."

"My brother John is a geologist."

"Great profession. I bet living so close he knows all about the formations."

"This might have been the inspiration because we all would come over here for picnics and I remember Papa talking to the boys and explaining lots of things about different areas."

"And you didn't listen."

"Well, I was younger and usually stayed with my mother. I'm not sure rocks would have interested me."

"This has been another lovely day," he said as he kissed her hand. He turned and said passionately, "Chris where have you been all of my life. Please tell me that there is no one else in your life. And please tell me that you are not in love with anyone."

She was surprised and found it difficult to answer. But she did softly. "No, I'm not in love with anyone," she replied softly. Her words were softened as he turned her head and kissed her soft lips. "Then be in love with me."

The smile that was on her face faded. Why does he tease, she thought? This man is from such a different world. He can't be interested in me. Anyway we just met. He probably tells every girl the same thing. She could only think of what her father had said. And . . . how can someone fall in love so quickly. She and Brian had been together for many years before they fell in love.

Realizing she did not answer he said, "Shall we go before the dinner crowd gets any bigger." But in his heart he was totally sincere.

♥

Twilight, dusk and early darkness were upon them as they reach her big stone house. The little light guiding her home was not on, that meant Papa Zeller had not retired for the evening. She asked Dan, "Would you like one last coffee, tea, hot chocolate. Papa is probably in the library and you can say hello again."

"I'd like that, how about tea."

Dan stopped briefly to say hello to her father. Then he followed her to the kitchen where they enjoyed their tea.

Dan said, "I should be going because I have to sort out gear for tomorrow and be rested for the interview. We have had a busy day and will probably sleep well tonight. I'll come out after the interview."

"That will be fine. And could I fix a picnic basket?" He thought that was a good idea.

She walked with him to the front door. Far out of sight of her father he turned and took her in his arms and touched her mouth with his fingers and parted her soft pink lips and placed his lips upon hers and kissed her long and lovingly several times. She wanted to be more responsive, but there were lingering emotions that would not go away.

"I really meant what I said earlier. I know myself well enough to recognize and know the reality of my feelings. Please be with me. Tomorrow, the old mill, it's not far."

As she nodded an okay, he turned and walked briskly to his car. Christina watched from the big window. The little red tail light faded into the dark as one had many times before.

The big window had witnessed years of emotions for all the family members. It was there someone watched for their loved one, a brother, mother or papa, a friend to arrive. It was there they all watched for the school bus. Daisy too learned she could look out when she sensed or heard a car in the drive. When Christina first started watching from the window she had to stand on a little stool to see out. And it was there that she had said goodbye to Brian too many times to count. Now she watched Dan go, happily knowing she would see him tomorrow. Another day of their friendship could make it stronger . . . or . . .

♥

As Dan drove away he too was having mixed thoughts.

I say something and she is happy and responsive, I say something else and she withdraws from me and even from herself. It seems to happen so fast I'm not quite sure what I say that causes this reaction. I do know when I talk about loving her it occurs.

He could definitely feel a barrier between them. Although it was a new friendship and love, and she seemed warm and open, but something or someone was creating a shadow. What could it be? Is there someone else? As he drove into the night he felt determined to find the answer.

♥

Christina quickly gave her papa a good night kiss and went to her bedroom. She stood silent and alone in her dark room. Her thoughts were encompassing but not deep. So quickly this friendship had unsettled her emotions, but also stirred her feelings. He makes me feel so relaxed she thought. When he touches, it stirs me inside. When he holds my hand he makes me feel that we belong. But my love for Brian had grown for years and now this person is here for three days and he says he is in love with me. It can't be. Reality doesn't work this way.

She had not planned for these strange and mixed emotions. Actually she had not wanted an intrusion at this time. And too, she was afraid to believe him, for fear he was not sincere. Feelings for Brian were still very strong in her heart and there was no room for a new love. Tomorrow will be here . . . and . . . over . . . and he will be gone. I will not let it happen. I will not allow myself to be hurt again.

CHAPTER FOUR

♥

Christina was awake early and found many things around the house to keep her busy. She thought of last evening. Dan's loving words and his tender embrace were all part of this new day. It all seemed so wonderful, but she wasn't sure, it wasn't all but a dream. She had decided to put all her concerns to rest. Her mind was clear. She was determined not to fall for some passing whim.

As she was gathering things for the picnic basket, the telephone rang. As she answered, "Hi sweetheart, are you okay today. I'm back at the hotel and will be out soon. I'm looking forward being with you today," and they talked for a few more minutes.

As she put the phone down her body grew warm and then cold. She was almost fearful. Can I believe him or will the results be painful again?

Putting his words out of her mind she continued to prepare the food for the picnic. Her father would soon be home with the dogs. He always waited while they got their bath.

Near ten–thirty she saw Dan's blue car in the long tree–lined drive. She tried to relax as she went to the door to welcome him. The dogs, nice and clean, were there too.

His greeting to her was without words. He took her boldly in his arms and kissed her lovingly. She responded with cautious desire.

"You look rested today. Have you been busy?" he finally asked.

"But wait, how did your interview go?"

"Real good. I think I was smooth in my responses. Mr. Conlon stuck pretty much to the questions. Mostly talked about the books. My personal approach, things that were not in the book, my remembrances, how particular incidents affected me."

"I can't wait to see it and so sorry that you can't be here to watch it with me. It will be great to have an actual author on the program. Most of the time it is two people discussing a book. But to have a real author, a real person will be special. Even more special it being you."

"You're too sweet. Yeah, I have to work a portion of every day for the next two weeks, so I will miss it. And your morning."

"I worked on school things. I do some work every day. Also I have been working on Christmas things for my little nieces."

"How many nieces do you have?"

"Four little ones, ages six and under and two older. It is easy, the little ones like dolls. I try to get most things made during the summer. Once school starts there isn't a lot of extra time."

"Do you prepare new work every year?"

"Yes, I change things around. It keeps me motivated and keeps them from copying."

"Sounds like a good idea. These guys look good today. They even smell good," he said referring to the dogs that stood happily by waiting for attention.

She laughed, "Papa took them to Stover's earlier for their bath."

They're so big. I'm glad they like me."

"Basically they are very gentle, but I've seen them excited a few times. It's nice they're here, when Papa is gone visiting, I'm not alone. Way out here in the country it can get lonesome. They're good company. They both bark if someone strange is around."

"Where does your father go?"

"Mostly to visit my brothers, sometimes he might be away for a few day consulting."

"Is that picnic ready that you agreed to make?" he asked as he smiled.

"Everything is in the basket. It's still in the kitchen."

"Let me get it," he offered. She led the way through the large house to the kitchen. "Here's the basket."

"You did need me to carry it," he laughed. "Full of good things. I'm hungry already."

"The mill is about an hour, maybe less. Are you going to take pictures too? After that we can find a place for our picnic."

"Yes I am going to take pictures, because I haven't been up there in a long time. I hear they have fixed it up and that it's very nice."

With basket in hand they started for the door. Christina called the dogs. "They have to go outside. Papa went over to the stables again, but he will be back soon." They went casually to his car.

♥

Christina was apprehensive. She enjoyed Dan's company and their intellectual exchange, but she did not want to be confronted with anything as serious as falling in love. If he insisted on an answer or reply she would have to change the subject again. She could not tell him she was afraid to fall in love again, especially with a person so far removed from her world. She thought he would be away on long assignments and I would be alone. She could not comprehend how she would fit into his life style. Also she felt she could not rush into anything until her feelings for Brian were at a resting place in her heart.

The day was warm and the drive pleasant. Christina soon relaxed as the conversation was casual and full of laughs. Dan is so much fun and easy to be with, she thought, if only he would let things happen naturally and forget about hurrying into a romance. It is just too soon for such a commitment.

They soon arrived at the mill and he had not mentioned his intensions again.

He gathered his camera and equipment and they walked toward the complex. "There seems to be quite a few people here even though it is a week day," he said as he handed her one of his bags.

"Do you always travel this well–equipped?" she asked.

"This is light," and he laughed. "We will have many good pictures, for my backdrops, and for your writing assignments."

"I can use them for fact or fiction writing."

The big, red, barn–shaped building was the main attraction of this ten acre country village. There are several other smaller buildings that represented life in an earlier time. A country kitchen, a blacksmith, textile shop were among those open. Other buildings were still being worked on and would be ready by the following spring. The slow grind of the water wheel also was symbolic of a slower time. Many colorful flower gardens and neatly trimmed grass added to the country beauty. It had been a joint effort of restoration by several historical societies in the western part of the state.

"I'd rather not have people in these pictures so I'll have to work quickly. I'm going to work outside first."

As they circled the large structure, Dan decided on a starting point. "I'll relieve you of that bag," he said to her as he took it and kissed her quickly on the lips. She smiled with pleasure.

First he took black and white photos and then he changed equipment for color. Chris watched as Dan worked and while he worked he talked. He told her about every angle he intended to capture, every color he needed to balance. He considered every facet, shade and light, size and shape.

As Christina took pictures she thought how she could use them for her writing assignments. The obvious was a pioneer story. It could be a frame for the theme of struggle. Physical and mental struggle. Weaving. Sewing clothes and blankets for warmth. Tending of a vegetable garden and preparing food for the winter. Caring for animals that were life sustaining for a family. Working in fields. Safe from intruders.

The emotional struggle which was mostly silent and perhaps more powerful. Disease. Would there be medicine? The wait to see if an illness would pass or take a loved one completely. Incorporate how a mother or father would cope. Also the elements of nature, welcoming spring only to have a flood. Welcoming the cooler weather only to have feet of snow. How so much could be accomplished with so little, called for a family to be very creative. This little village that we're taking pictures of was their whole world at that time. Her last thought was this will make a good exercise in writing.

While she was thinking, she watched Dan without him knowing. In his denim shorts and plaid shirt he gave a different appearance, but he was still the Dan she had just met a few days ago. It was almost like watching him that first night at Bellamy House. His every actions and words brought a smile to her face. She thought he is very desirable. What can this relationship bring? She questioned herself.

"They did a nice job of restoration. This is the first time in a long time that I have been here. You too?" he asked.

"Not in a long time. My sister–in–law and I were going to come over one day, but we didn't have enough time. I'm glad you suggested it. It is very nice and going to be better when they finish all the buildings," she added happily.

"Let's check out the interior of the big red building," he said.

The inside was graced with furniture of the period. Many hours of handwork gave a homey feeling. There were hooked rugs and quilted objects that were old, although some were reproductions. Dishes on the table and bread in the oven capture a ready-to-live in feeling.

He motioned to her from a distance and pointed upstairs. She nodded in agreement.

As expected the upper level was bedrooms. Each had been decorated with different colors and attractive accessories relating to times. Quilts, pottery and more hooked rugs were all part of the décor.

Chris examined and admired the beautiful crafted items with care. "They're all so lovely."

"Do you make things like this?"

"I do a few things, mostly I paint. When there is time."

"You're a painter? How interesting. Oil, water color?"

"Mostly oil, and I was just thinking the Old Range Bridge would make a good subject."

"Let's do that. You can set up your easel and I can relax with a book on a blanket nearby."

"You would probably finish your book before I finished my painting."

No, Dan thought, I would be looking at you more than reading.

"Will you show me some of the paintings you've done," he asked in a sincere manner.

"Sure, if you really want."

"You have many talents, do you cook, because I love to eat," and he laughed.

"I get out a recipe and follow it. Papa likes what I fix," she was pleased to report as they both laughed.

"I'd like to take a couple more of the water wheel and I noticed they have picnic tables. We can have our picnic lunch."

"Yes, we need nourishment after so much walking," she added.

"I'll trade this equipment for the picnic basket and we'll take one of those trails off into the sunset and eat," he said humorously.

♥

Again she watched this handsome attractive man walk boldly to his car. What a beautiful three days, four counting the reception, she thought. But it is all happening so fast. I want to come to love on my own, not be forced. Feelings for Brian also must be entirely gone and I must know that Dan is sincere, she thought again. As she watched him return she grew warm with the thought of him near her, very near her.

He took her hand and they followed the path into a wooded area. "The remainder of this day I'm going to devote, without distraction, to you, my dear Christina," he assured her.

They walked slowly enjoying the trees. The path was wide and the woods were neat, almost groomed. Tall trees hovered over them creating a canopy above their heads. The warm summer air was broken by a slight breeze. A few sparrows flitted by, but most of the birds were somewhere else on this summer afternoon. Only the gentle rushing of the nearby stream could be heard.

"It is so peaceful here and nothing could make me happier than being married to you."

Chris rather embarrassed was lost for words. "You shouldn't treat this matter so lightly."

"I'm not treating it lightly. I would never do this about something as serious as a life together called marriage."

She was always hesitant about being loved or when he spoke about marriage. She could have said something to distract or change the subject, but she withdrew. It wasn't just an evasion but she seemed to create a barrier.

He realized it wasn't time to talk about this matter. I don't want to rush or destroy any feelings that have already been developed. I will stop talking, was his final thought.

They walked on a little further. "There's a table under the maple tree," he said as he pointed in its direction.

"It's perfect."

They made their way to the table and opened the basket. Tablecloth first then the food.

"I should have brought a bottle of wine. I had a small Christmas party last year and someone brought this Chateau de Lords and it has been one of my favorites ever since. It is not expensive but really nice. Do you like white wine or red?"

"I do like white better than red," she added.

"What did you fix?" He peeked in the basket and sat down next to her at the table.

"Chicken salad sandwiches, they're little, cupcakes, they're little too, a plate of apples, oranges and cheddar, and some juice," she said slowly as she removed the food from the basket and arranged it on the tablecloth.

"A feast!" he exclaimed happily.

"You're serious about what you eat. I have definitely noticed."

"I eat lots of fruits, vegetables, not much meat. Do you cook?" she inquired of him.

"Very little. I'm home one day and gone the next. Sometimes I work late. It is not practical to keep too much food around. If I know I am going to be home for several days, then I might get some food and I do get long stretches of time that I work at the studio, so I eat at home."

There was lull in their conversation but not a lull in Christina's thoughts.

"Thinking how hungry you are?" Dan asked.

"No, I was thinking about what you said when you were preparing your scene and how easily it could be applied to painting. I have to find my light source, the moon, sun. I balance a tree or a hill. Very important, where I place little dabs of color. All of these little things make a whole."

"A wonderful observation and it certainly whets my appetite to see your paintings."

"Our arts are so closely intertwined, all arts. I was also thinking how I could use this setting for a writing assignment." And she told Dan her thoughts.

"That is quite an outline for your students. All art can also be applied to the concepts you mentioned. Struggling to get the right words on paper or color on canvas. It is a small struggle compared to pioneer times."

"In college I took this drawing and painting class of human anatomy. What a problem I had with faces. I could not express any emotion. And the professor did not like me."

"He didn't like you? How did you know?"

"He told me so. He said that I shouldn't be there because I was not an art student and that he didn't like me for taking up space that should go to someone else."

"He told you that? You find all kinds."

"It doesn't matter. I only wanted to develop different forms of art but that didn't quite happen."

They continued talking about many things as they enjoyed the lunch that Christina had prepared.

After they finished eating he helped her get things back into the basket. "I'll put the basket in the car and let's walk over to the stream, creek or whatever it is. I have been listening to it ripple, now I want to see it," he said.

"I have been listening too. It is such a peaceful sound. It could lull you right to sleep. I was thinking about what you said yesterday, its nature's music.

Such a contrast, this is so soft and yesterday the falls so loud and not missing a beat."

"I remember," he responded with a smile.

He is always smiling she thought. I do believe he is a happy person. That makes everything so much better.

He was back and had a blanket tucked under his arm. They followed the path a bit farther and then walked to the water. "A good spot to enjoy the stream for a while." Dan spread the blanket on the grass and draped one end over a large log.

"Are you involved in any drama?"

"Sort of, last year they had three performances. We're lucky we have a drama teacher three half days a week."

"That's a nice addition."

"What the English department does, we have after school gatherings of the casts and we explain the play and we also help them study lines in small groups. All the teachers help out. I don't know what they will be doing this year."

They talked a while longer and then just relaxed, watching the rushing water in the shallow bed readying itself for the big wheel at the mill. It leaped and bounced happily between the large rocks. This water had searched from far away in time for a peaceful end, an end, where it can rest as a gentle lake or a sleeping pond.

He gently took her hand as they sat by the water mesmerized in feeling and thought.

They closed their eyes and surrendered themselves to nature. Chris softly laid her head on

Dan's shoulder. She felt his hand relax in hers and she though, I believe he dozed off.

The rays of the falling sun made its way through the leaves and the shadows danced upon their face. After a while the contrast of light and shade brought Dan to gain his composure. "Did we just fall sleep?" he said as he chuckled slightly.

"I did," Christina said slowly as just waking up.

"This was another wonderful day. The food, the great outside and most of all being with you. Here we are at the beginning of our life together." He smiled as he gazed into her eyes.

"We had better go. I don't know what time this closes. Don't want to get locked in and have to stay in one of those bedrooms on the top floor," again he laughed.

As they walked to the car he asks, "What would you like to do for the rest of the evening? It is still early."

"Well. The stores are open until eight. The gallery is open till eight. A movie, the drive–in," she slowly list the few things.

"A drive-in, that's perfect. We won't have to get dressed up. I don't even get to the indoor movie very often. That would be a treat!"

We can go by your house and you can freshen up. Then we can stop at the hotel and I will freshen up. And that will be good timing," he said slowly planning as he spoke. He looked at her for approval.

"That's fine."

♥

They drove to her home and while she freshened up Dan played ball outside with Daisy and Henry. On to the hotel where Dan was staying so he could do the same. "Come on up while I make myself respectable."

Dan went into the bath and came out a few minutes later without a shirt. Oh my Christina thought, as she relaxed in the big chair, he's so beautiful. Dan got a clean shirt out of his suitcase and slipped it on, all the while talking to her.

"I'm ready." He reached for her hand. He took her in his arms and again gave her that loving look. This moment she returned the expression.

She broke the silence. "Let's go. Want to pick up a hamburger and Coke along the way and we can eat before the movie."

"You will have to guild me to the drive-in. I hope there is one close," he responded.

"Yes, actually there is one on the way home."

Dan and Chris left the hotel, picked up their food and on to the drive–in. They arrived early enough so they could eat before the movie started. There were several movies to choose from and they decided on one that recently was being shown at the drive-ins, *M * A * S * H*. They both thought it would be entertaining because they had heard good reviews from their friends.

Hamburgers finished just in time for the starting of the movie. Dan pushed the seat back and moved over near Christina. He put his arm around her and there they sat watching the movie very attentively to catch all the humorous and serious dialog of the actors. He whispered, "Just like high school."

She giggled and nodded yes.

But for Dan it was way beyond high school. He felt he had fallen very much in love with Christina, almost at first sight. It was a very strong feeling, a feeling that he had never known before. He had dated girls and had a couple close relationships, but this was different. He was totally sure that he wanted Christina for his wife, lover and soul mate for the end of his time. Moreover, he planned to work diligently to that end. He wanted to do everything right. He wanted her to know that he was sincere and would be devoted and faithful forever.

When the movie was over he kissed her once very softly. "I'll get you home. I don't want to get on the bad side of your father," he said jokingly.

She laughed too, "Papa knows I'm a big girl."

As they drove to her home they talked and laughed about the movie that they had just seen. They both enjoyed it. "Also about tomorrow I believe I mentioned I was going to drive up and visit my parents for the day. If you have no plans, I would like for you to go with me. I talked to Mom yesterday morning and told her that I would ask you and she said that would be wonderful. And I would like very much for you to meet them, and them to meet you."

"Oh my!" she exclaimed. "Meet your parents so soon, I hardly know you."

"Sometime it doesn't take long to know someone," he responded.

"No, I don't have plans. Are you sure you want me to go?"

"I'm sure," he said "It takes about two hours and mom and dad are pretty easy to be with, at least I think so. And I won't have to drive alone. And we can keep talking about all these things we never run out of words about." He gently kept trying to convince her to go with him.

Finally and reluctantly she said she would go.

Joyfully he went on with plans. "I could pick you up around ten. We would be there by twelve. Mom will have a big lunch. We'll visit and I'll show you around. If we leave by four, we'll be at your house around six and I could be back in the big city by nine."

"You didn't just make this up. Sounds like you had this planned all along," she said as she laughed.

He too laughed, "This was plan A." He continued smiling. "And there was no plan B."

He reached for her hand and they laughed together.

Chris thought, he sounds sincere, but when he leaves will he still have the same feelings. For now I will just listen and not react.

"The next day is Friday, but I have to work for the next three days. Some of these events that I have to work are not just nine to five."

When they reached her home, they could see the little light that was to guide Christina home one more time. "Your papa always leaves the light on for you? He seems like a great dad."

"He couldn't be better and has always been here for all of us, mother and my brothers. And now he has his own life and I have mine, but we look after each other."

"He's retired?" Dan questioned.

"Yes, about two years ago. He owned Zeller Architecture. It was his father's before. Grandfather started the business when he finished school. It grew and my father too decided that he wanted to become an architect and joined the firm and became a partner. When my grandfather passed it became my father's. But none of my brothers or me wanted to follow so he sold it to four of the guys that worked there."

"Was he sad when none of his boys especially, did not want to follow in the family business," Dan asked.

"Well, I think he was but he realized that we had to do what we wanted," she replied. "And yet they all work in a field that requires lots of math."

"But not you."

"No, I went for the more gentle approach. My mother's side, literature, poetry, painting. But Papa does a lot of classical reading. I know you have only seen him behind a newspaper, but he reads all the time. He likes reading about ancient architecture. We read together in our library, especially in the winter."

This set Dan to thinking. Would she leave her father? Or was she harboring something deeper? Why was this beautiful girl seemingly content to live and work out here far from the greater activities of life?

He walked with her to the door and he held her near and kissed her lightly. "Until tomorrow, ten."

Chris went in and watched from the big window as the little red light on the back of his car got smaller and smaller and then was gone completely. One more time someone had left her to be alone. But quickly her thoughts were of tomorrow. His parents! Oh my gosh! With that heavy thought she was off to her bedroom. And she slept well.

CHAPTER FIVE

♥

Christina woke to a bright and sunny August day. Quickly she remembered that she was going with Dan for a brief visit with his mother and father. She joined her papa for coffee and she told him where she was going for the day.

"Meeting the parents, that's important," was his reply.

"I know Papa, but last evening he just kept giving me reason after reason why he wanted me to go," she responded with emphasis. Softening her tone, "Papa he is so nice."

Her father could tell she had found a little softness toward Dan. That he liked, because he felt that she had let Brian, although gone, control too much of her life. She had refused too many dates and traced too many steps that she and Brian had taken. Maybe this is the one person that will bring her completely out of this web of loneliness that she has woven around herself. Then he said a little prayer to himself, if this happens don't let her be hurt again.

"I'm going over to Ellen's this morning. Her back step needs fixing. Tell Dan I will see him when you get back this evening. I'll be home early to take care of the dogs."

Ellen is a dear family friend. Her brother owned a large contracting business and Zeller Architecture did a lot of work for them. She lives about twenty minutes from their home and he rather looks after her. She never married and when her mother passed, John and Lydia were there for her, as were other friends. As time goes by, he and Ellen spend more and more time together.

But, Christina felt that her papa would not become serious about any lady as long as she lived at home And she felt like she would be there for a long time.

♥

Christina readied herself for the day with Dan and his parents. He arrived promptly at ten. Daisy and Henry met him as they did the days before. They did not bark. They were becoming well acquainted and they liked him. As Christina was making her way from the back of the house, she called, "Come on in, I just went to get my bag."

Dan heard and did just that. As he said good morning he took her in his arms and kissed her lightly. "You're beautiful this morning as always. I like your hair pulled back. Ready for the ride? I called mom this morning before I checked out and told her that you had consented to come along with me." What else Dan told his mother was how he had fallen in love with Christina and that she does not quite respond. She was reluctance at times, but he would be determined.

The ride to his parents' home was uneventful. They chatted, laughed and had serious moments too. One thing he asked about the earlier part of her summer before he had met her.

"On nice days, weather that is, I went to the Grange and rode. They have some well–groomed paths and trails and a nice track. I especially like one of the horses. It is a wonderful time to reflect. We have never had horses but my grandfather did. Papa said he was too busy with kids to have horses too. The Grange is not far and we all spent a lot of time over there. Papa knows the owner real well."

She also told him of her visit to her brother and sister–in–law in San Francisco. "We had a marvelous time. They both work so I did a lot of sight–seeing during the day. Their girls are ten and eleven and I took them everywhere with me. It was a nice treat for them because they were just out of school. Then in the afternoon we would go home and fix dinner together. It would be ready when John and Rachel got home. They are the sweetest girls. Little ladies. I'm not sure who had more fun them or me."

"Did you ride the trolley car?"

"No the lines were too long. Anyway I don't like hills. The one weekend I was there, we all drove up north for the day."

"You went to the Fisherman's Wharf?"

"The girls took me that day because they had been there quite a few times. I enjoyed, they enjoyed."

"I was there twice, briefly, once on assignment and on the way back from Vietnam, when I worked for *World*. Didn't get to see much either time. It is a beautiful city but you can't help but think about earthquakes. How long were you there?"

"Ten days. I can just spend the summers visiting my brothers and be very occupied. I like all my sisters–in–law very much."

"And your other brothers?"

"Jim and Dave both live in St. Louis and I was there for a week earlier in the summer. Their children are younger. Last Easter Papa and I went to Pittsburgh. Bill and Karen live there. So this year we got to all of them. I believe they are all planning to be here for Christmas."

"I can't wait to see Bill again. That is going to be special. See what he remembers. And why we drove out here. I laugh every time I think about this whole thing." And he paused, "Now all you need is a husband and children to complete this marvelous family. And we're going to have some catching up to do."

Chris became painfully silent and Dan knew he had struck the wrong tone. She gazed out the passenger window and into the distant morning and thought to herself, it would be just that way if Brian was here. Her thoughts strayed further and further. Her face grew bland and her eyes a bit glassy.

"I'm sorry if I upset you but, I'm not sorry that I said what I did. I want to be the one."

She realized after a few moments that she was ignoring Dan and quickly came back to her present self.

He definitely knew there was something standing between them. She hadn't been able to hide her feelings very well over the last few days. Dan decided to change the subject. "What else have you done exciting this summer?"

"Not too exciting, as I mentioned before, Christmas presents. Last year was a big time for the little girls. Papa and I made three little doll houses and some of the furniture. Well Papa did most of the work. A chance to apply his architectural skills, even in miniature. I think he enjoyed making them especially for his granddaughters. I made rugs and curtains. We bought most of the furniture. I made little dolls. The girls were absolutely beside themselves. They were so surprised. The little five year old thought she had to leave it here at papa's house. It was quite a scene. Papa applied his gentle skills and got her under control. He made Julie and Katie one several years ago when they were about four and five."

A long pause and she asked, "Do you have a hobby?"

"I take pictures," he said in a jovial manner. "No I don't have any real hobbies. My brownstone is not very big. Also my time off, other than planned vacation, is usually short, so I don't have time to get involved in large projects. I do read a lot and that is a great pleasure for me and it is something that I can take with me. Although in the past several years I have been writing more. It started out as a journal and notes to go with photos, and then it evolved into impressions and story ideas and some poetry. Whatever comes to mind. It's only for me. It is relaxing and an escape. In my business there are always technical books and magazines to read. I have to keep up on all the new stuff."

"Your brother in San Francisco?" he asked.

"John is my oldest brother."

"I don't remember him, we probably never met."

"Bill, Karen is his wife. And they have two little girls. He met her in college. He's a research engineer and works for General Electric. She is an elementary teacher and on leave until the girls get a little older."

"I can hardly believe that I saw you once running with your dogs. That makes one believe in fate. It was destiny for us to meet again. It has to mean something." What Dan was saying that he felt they were meant for each other and there is a very distinct plan for their life together.

He didn't usually believe in fate, but there were too many things to dismiss the wonderful thought.

Although attentive to what Dan was saying, he could see a distance in her demeanor. Was she just going back in time with him or was she thinking of what fate had brought to her.

These little vignettes of words and thoughts carried them closer to Dan's folks.

"We're almost there," he said, and a few more turns and they were.

His parents were waiting for them on the front porch Hugs, handshakes and introducing Chris started this great day together.

"Come on in," his mother said to them. "Your dad and I just finished preparing the biggest lunch ever. We knew you would be hungry after that long ride."

"Mom, that is so sweet of you and dad, but we didn't spend much energy just riding. Although we spent a lot of energy talking," he said as he smiled at Christina.

"Let's eat now and we can show Christina around later. Is that okay?" his mother suggested.

They gathered around the table to enjoy the lunch his mom and dad had prepared. Dan told his parents about some of his recent assignments and the reception at Bellamy House. "It certainly was the best reception because I met Chris there," he said as he gave her a quick wink and a smile.

He also went on to tell them about the TV interview and when it would be aired.

"You mentioned London, when are you going?" His mother asked.

Chris perked up because he had not mentioned London to her. "October, I don't remember the exact date," he replied.

What his mother didn't ask, was he going to see Caroline while there She knew they had been more than friends but things never quite came together for them. Maybe this time would be different. He had met Caroline about two years ago and there had been a long distant relationship. She had visited Dan twice and he had been there several times. But now Christina had come into his life and he expressed his love although only a short time had passed, his feelings had not waned. After lunch Dan's father suggested they take a walk and he would show Dan and Chris his flower and vegetable gardens. His father Ralph and Chris walked together in the garden path as he talked briefly about what he had planted and what came back from the previous year. Dan and his mother lagged behind in deep conversation about the reception and a few old acquaintances that had attended.

"And London," she inquired. "How long will you be there?"

"No more than a month, perhaps less. Things can go good and my time will be short or maybe longer."

"Have you heard from Caroline? Are you planning to see her?"

"No, I haven't heard from her in six months and I have no plans to see her. Anyway, Mom, I am so enamored with Chris I don't know what to do. I feel like a kid in high school. This has never happened to me before."

"She is very sweet and she seems to compliment you well," his mother acknowledged.

"Do you remember her family? They have a big farm off Lake Road. Her father owned Zeller Architect."

"No, I don't remember, your father might."

"She has four brothers. Our school had a debate and I was down there. And I went to their home with her brother Bill and saw her with her dogs. She must have been about twelve years old and me probably seventeen. It's such a coincidence. I told her that it had to mean something, but she just ignored me."

"That is rather interesting, you were at her home once. We were there such a short time. Anyway it is nice that you have found someone that you know something about. She lives closer than London."

"We had better catch up to them," Dan continued.

It was a beautiful summer afternoon, not too hot. After a tour of the gardens they settled on the front porch and continued their lively conversation. They asked Chris about school and Dan about past and future assignments. They all seem to be enjoying the visit and the time went by too fast.

Dan was the one to suggest they begin the trek to Christina's and then on to the big city and his brownstone. "I have about four hours driving. This week is not scheduled well. I have to work tomorrow, Saturday and Sunday. And then without rest my week begins again." He didn't seem to mind for he smiled while he was talking.

Loving goodbyes and they were on their way. The ride home was much the same as the ride earlier.

They arrived to find the dogs waiting.

"Come in for a few minutes, at least stretch," Chris offered.

"While you fix coffee I'll say hello to your father."

Dan found him in the library and they chatted a few minutes and then he went to the kitchen to have a quick coffee with Christina.

"I'll fix you a sandwich and there is potato salad in the fridge. You won't have to stop to eat. Unless you want to eat now. Lunch, as wonderful and big as it was, but a long time ago."

"If I can leave by seven, I'll be okay."

"A sandwich will take two minutes and it will be ready."

"Okay and you are too sweet and thoughtful."

Christina made Dan a big one and herself a small one.

They sat across from each other at the large harvest table enjoying one more meal together.

"This has been a very special five days for me. I've never felt this way before. I'm going to come right to the point, I'm falling in love with you." He reached across the table and took her hand.

She seemed startled but not surprised because these days, Dan seemed to present himself as more than a date.

"We have to be sure of such feelings, we haven't known each other very long," she said softly.

Her thoughts went back to Brian and how long they had known each other before he said those words to her.

"I know," he said and then continued. "I'll be patient. I'll call you often and get together often so our feelings can grow." he said gently as he looked lovingly into her eyes. "And this is what I leave with you. In two weeks I have an assignment south of the big city. Maybe we can meet half way or something.

I'll think it out and let you know. Is your papa still in the library?" he asked as he ended his words of love to her.

"No, I think he went to the back garage. He cleans out a little at a time."

"On our way out, could I take one last peek at that beautiful room?"

"Sure," she answered.

Once in the library he closed the door and said, "Yes, it's a beautiful room but I just wanted to get you alone so I can hold you and kiss you one last time before I leave for home."

Face to face they gazed into each other's eyes. Dan placed his hand on her back and guided her close. His other hand in her hair and closer he wet her lips with his tongue and rolled it into her waiting mouth and he kissed her passionately. His hand went down her back and he pulled her to meet his body. She softened easily.

"A very special ending to the greatest time in my life. May this be only the beginning of our life together? I'll be on my way now."

They looked at each other with contented smiles, reeling from this closeness.

She walked to the car with him. Of course Daisy and Henry had to go with them. One last moment of closeness and then he was gone.

Christina went back into the house and watched him from the big window as he departed. His big blue car faded into the evening sunset and then out of sight.

She could hardly believe what these five days had brought. Meeting, being constantly together and then he tells me he loves me, she thought. What if I never see him again? What if I see him next weekend? She was totally overwhelmed. Well, I will deal with what happen when it happens, her thoughts continued.

Her father came back in the house and found her still standing by the big window. "Is he gone?" he asked.

"Yes," she replied softly still staring out the big window.

"Did you have a nice time today?" he asked.

"Yes," she said again softly, a little further in deep thought.

"Is everything okay Chris?" he asked as he sensed her distant reaction.

Quickly and happily she said, "Oh yes Papa, we had a very nice time today. His parents were very nice. He said he would call. If he does, okay, and if not, okay too. But we had a nice time all the days."

She did not tell her father what Dan had said to her because she was not quite ready to believe it herself. Time will be very important she thought.

For the remainder of the evening Chris busied herself and went to bed early. She read for a while, then turned out her light and lay quietly as the cool night breeze swirled about. It wasn't Dan she was thinking about, but Brian. His presence was still so very strong and she had loved him for so long. She felt the feelings for him would never be over. She slept well.

CHAPTER SIX

♥

Ending a perfect five days with a new love should have made Christina the happiest person ever, but her heart seemed still closed to that world. She did not know if Dan or anyone could open it wide enough for a new love to enter in. The dark shadow that Brian had cast would not fade from her life. It lingered in her memory. She often questioned, if she would ever be free to love again. The memory of those years together was just too strong to go away.

It had all happened one day when Brian found her in a most unsuspecting place, washing ponies at a local stable.

That moment forever created a vivid picture in Christina's memory. She was bending over washing a pony's foot. As she straightened up and looked over his back she came face to face with a young teen with a mass of golden blond curls and blue eyes. His boyish face tanned by the summer sun, broke into a smile. "Aren't you kind of small to be doing such heavy work?"

"No," she replied crisply. "I love it and I'm strong."

Christina had just finished eighth grade and would be going to Brigham High School in the fall. That summer she worked at the stables. She didn't receive any money and she didn't care, she just wanted to be around the horses and ponies. Her parents did not like her being there, but she so passionately begged, just for a few weeks. Christina usually got what she wanted within reason. Of course Papa Zeller knew the owner and knew he would watch out for her. Her job would be determined by the needs of the day. Some days she would have to put oats in the feeding bin, other days she would have to wash the ponies. And yes even clean the stables. She even took her own shovel.

This also meant that someone would have to drive her and pick her up. That summer there were four family members that could do that. John and Jim had been away at college but everyone was home for the summer, and of course mother and father were also available. So they worked it out, Christina would work at the stables a few hours a day and for a few weeks that summer.

That particular day Papa Zeller went for Christina and he recalls it so vividly. When she came out she was not alone. With her was a young teen boy a bit shorter than she—she was tall for her age—and he was guiding his bike.

Her words were, "Papa this is Brian and he is going home with me. Can we pleas put his bike in the back of the van?"

Papa had asked, "Why is he going home with you?" And what he thought but did not say, aren't there enough boys at your house already.

She proceeded to tell her papa this was her new friend she had met here this morning. He likes horses too. And he is going to Brigham next year.

Papa asked him where he lived and how he planned to get home. He had said he would ride his bike. Papa said, "That is a long way for you to ride."

Brian seated himself in the back and Christina in front with her papa. All the way home Chris leaned over the seat, facing Brian, and they talked and talked and talked.

I can't wait to go to high school . . . me too . . . what are you going to take . . . biology . . . me too . . . what else . . . I like stories, literature . . . I write poetry . . . me too . . . we can do our homework together . . . I have four brothers . . . that's a lot of brothers . . . you'll meet them they're all home . . . are they fun . . . sometimes . . . I have a sister . . . Do you have any sisters . . . no I have girlfriends . . . Papa did you see Brian's curls, aren't they cute . . . I'm going to cut them off before I go to school . . . no don't I like them . . . where did you go to grade school . . . Kendall Grade . . . I went to South Ridge . . . do you like to read . . . yes . . . what is your favorite book . . . I like them all . . . do you have a hobby . . . I sew with my mother, do you . . . my father died three years ago and I use his tools to make things . . . I made a bird house and it came out pretty good . . . I like to paint .

. . pictures . . . do you play sports . . . softball and I run track . . . I played volleyball in gym class but I just like to ride . . . me too . . . I can't wait to go to college . . . me too . . . where do you ride . . . over at the Grange . . . me too . . . I took riding lessons . . . mom said she couldn't afford for me to take lessons so I help out over there and get to ride . . . they taught me how so I could exercise the horses . . . we can ride together . . . that'll be fun . . . do you have a job . . . no I'm only fourteen . . . me too . . . we have two German shepherds . . . I like dogs right now mom says we can't afford a dog . . . can I play with yours . . . Chloe and Sable they like to play ball and run.

The drive home Christina and Brian did not stop talking. They discussed almost everything without reservations and totally uninhibited. It was innocence at its best.

Papa was rather amused and pretended not to listen, but he was. He did not have to ask any questions, their conversations told everything. He knew all about Brian and Brian knew all about Christina. By the time they were home he liked this young boy but also felt empathy for him. He seemed happy and stable although deprived by circumstance.

As well as listening to Christina and Brian, Papa Zeller ran his own thoughts. Could this be her first boyfriend? Oh my god my little girl is growing up. No not yet. She is too young to have a boyfriend.

This was her first indication of noticing another boy, other than her brothers. But for Christina and Brian it was pure friendship. They just happened to be of different gender. They found an almost instant liking for each other.

They reached home, they all got out and Christina called to Brian, come on in and meet my mother. Papa Zeller followed close behind. Filing into the kitchen, Christina, Brian and Papa Zeller, they stopped. Mother I have a new friend and can he stay for dinner. Her mother looked at her, then Brian and then at her husband whose expression was wide–eyed and puzzling. Papa was speechless and she could see from the expression he was not sure what was happening. Her mother surprised, but could not refuse because one of the boys often had a friend for dinner.

Christina took Brian into the library and they played music until dinner. Lydia and John had quite a discussion. This certainly happened fast and without warning.

One by one the Zeller boys arrived for dinner and there were questions. Who's that? What's your name? Brian with confidents had said I'm Christina's new friend. Heaven help us, another boy in the house. They expressed everything from whispers to laughs and jokes about Christina having a boyfriend. One by one mother or father hushed up the fun without it being too obvious. Brian and Christina were totally unaware of her brother's silly remarks and they continued getting to know each other. After dinner Brian thanked Christina's mother for inviting him to dinner. "I really liked the cake."

Lydia Zeller was impressed at his courtesy and being at ease with such a big family and mostly boys.

After dinner Christina and Brian talked on the front porch and as the sun was setting, she ask if she could get Brian's bike out of the van. Papa Zeller had said, "Don't you think that it's too far for you to ride. It will be dark soon."

"Not if I hurry," he replied kindly.

"Come on, leave your bike in the van and Chris and I will drive you home."

One night, I can do this papa thought. But this was only the beginning and one of the many times Brian was driven home.

While they were gone the boys got a lecture from their mother. Especially Dave and Jim, they had led the frivolities at the dinner table.

That was the beginning and from that day on Brian was at the Zellers more than he was at home.

She was fourteen and he was fourteen, and from that day at the stables they belong to each other. Papa Zeller felt he had acquired a fifth son.

Their life together had begun with fun. They both loved to ride and that they did often, his golden locks wiggling in the quick passing wind and her long soft brown hair flowing behind. Chloe and Sable often ran along beside.

One spring they planted a flower garden at Christina's house. They dug a new bed, bought plants and after much arguing about where certain ones should be planted they managed to get it done. Through the years they tended it together, planting new and welcoming old. Today from the library window the garden is still blooming. Not with the same flowers but the outline of rocks that she and Brian laid still remains. Christina plants alone every year and tends it faithfully.

One day they exchanged locks of hair, so part of each other could be near when they were apart.

Christina snipped a strand of her soft brown hair and with a piece of red string, that she just happened to have in her pocket, tied those strands tightly together, made a bow and placed it in Brian's hand and closed it tightly. That day Brian placed a lock of his golden curls on her ring finger. Without words their belonging to each other was sealed. Although they both knew that long before.

Often they walked in the woods to find and identify mushrooms for their biology class. They often walked in the woods at dusk and listened to the lone thrush call forth the evening. Often Christina would read Brian a new poem that she had written.

They had scheduled many of the same classes in school and obviously did their homework together and Brian had to be driven home by Christina's mom. The proms—no one ever considered asking Christina, because everyone knew she was with Brian. They graduated together and Papa Zeller had one big party for both families at his home.

As the years passed they grew taller especially Brian. From early teens to mature teens and they went on to become two beautiful young adults.

They both went to different colleges, but neither far from home and soon as classes were over for the week they would rush home to be together. When they visited each other's college it was evident to their friends why they never dated anyone at their school. Everyone knew it was a very special relationship, and that it was.

Brian had been her sole comfort when her mother died. Her brothers and their wives had to leave soon after the funeral and her father was so distraught that he could hardly be of solace, even to his beloved daughter.

Their life that had begun as fun turned to fondness, as the years passed their fondness turned to love. Neither quite sure just when that had happened, but along the way it did. It had been the purest kind of love and for both—it was the first and the only. It was going to last forever. From somewhere in the beginning there had never been any doubt in either of their minds that someday they would be married and this they planned. Their plans for a life together were near completion, home and many children, all the things that make memories to grow old with. There was no need to hurry. They thought youth and time were theirs, but what they did not know that time was short for their love together. One day Brian would interrupt all they had hoped for and leave Christina alone with those empty plans. Their life together would divide, each to take a different path into the future.

Christina had been devastated and she had never forgiven him for leaving her life so empty. The promise of a beautiful future whisked away in one ugly moment.

Often she felt it had not happened, and he would return and they could go forth without interruption. As time passed she gradually accepted the fact that he could not return. Yet there were times when she waited and watched by the big window, hoping she would awake and find it all a bad dream. Her love for him had never found rest. It lived to haunt her and hold her to the past. It refused to take its place as a memory in her heart.

CHAPTER SEVEN

♥

Morning broke with brilliant sunshine. Not long after Christina was up and dressed, the phone rang. It had to be Dan she thought.

"Good morning my dear, I miss you already. Did you sleep well after the five day whirlwind?"

"I really did," she happily replied. "I really did."

"I have a full schedule for the next several weeks. I would not have committed to that, but it was before I met you. But it will run out soon and I can schedule to have my weekends free. Then we can get together more."

"I'm a little busy right now too. School will start shortly and we have to meet a few days before the students arrive to see that everything is in order. I have a room that I must fix up a bit. Little stuff."

"I checked my schedule for the weekend of the twenty–first and twenty–second and I will be working at Elmwood Stadium at an antique car show. As you probably know, that is on the south end of the city. About a half-hour is the village of Scotia. I think it's about an hour from your house. I was wondering if we could meet there for Saturday dinner and spend the night. Sunday I have to leave early and be at the stadium before the crowds come, but at least we can have dinner and spend the night. How does that sound?"

"That would be okay. I do have a meeting Friday, but that's all. Papa will be here to take care of the dogs."

"The inn at Scotia is the Hitching Post. It is quite large, it's kind of an inn, bed and breakfast combined. I was there last year for a magazine group meeting."

"I know where it is. We go through there on the way to the Shire," she replied.

"Would you be kind enough to call and make reservations for the night and dinner also? Put them in my name. If they ask tell them you are my secretary. But we know you are much more."

She said as she laughed. "I'll do that."

The conversation continued trivial but warm. After a few moments he said, "Dear Christina, I have to go to work. I'll call you every few days and till then. Know that I do love you."

She wanted to respond but something held her back from too saying those words, especially for the first time on the phone.

"We'll have a nice time, even if it is short," she said.

With that they said goodbye.

♥

The weekend passed and so the week. Chris had made reservations for the night and dinner at the inn. She also packed a small bag for it was only for overnight. It would be nice to be with Dan again. Maybe I can return his love, she pondered. But I must know that he is sincere and be at peace with my feelings for Brian. I do not feel I should be rushed to make any decision, about myself, about Dan or about Brian.

Dan called Thursday and his plans had not changed and she said that everything at the inn was confirmed.

Saturday, after lunch she said goodbye to her papa and the dogs and was on her way. The drive to Scotia was pleasant. Her thoughts were about Dan and their relationship. They were neutral thoughts. She was not asking herself profound questions or searching for rational answers, she was simply thinking about what had happened and what had been said between them. This will all work out naturally if it is meant to be, a calm voice in her head reassured her.

The little village of Scotia came into view. Most of the stores and restaurants were located on the main street. It was a quiet village with a strong impression of the past. The general store and quaint tavern were a few that had survived from the olden days. In the center of the main street was a large fountain and it was surrounded with summer flowers. Although the village was pleasant it offered nothing special so it was not a tourist attraction. It had remained quiet and sedate as life around it moved forward.

It was early afternoon and was not expected at the inn until after three o'clock. She parked her car and did some shopping. There were a few stores that interested her, a small boutique and the bookstore. She bought a scarf and a pair of earrings and from the bookstore a magazine.

The country inn was located several blocks off Main Street. She parked her car and went to check them both in. The large reception room had several large couches, end tables and was attractively decorated. The fireplace was lovely, but no fire was needed at this time of the year, and of course she noted the paintings on the walls.

She knew Mr. Haddonfield by his name tag and she announced herself and that Mr. Halloran would be here between five and six o'clock. She also confirmed dinner at seven.

"You'll be in room six and Mr. Halloran will have suite eleven." He said as he showed Christina to her room.

From her room upstairs she could see much of the spacious grounds, the walkway to the pond, small groups of trees and many colorful flowers scattered throughout.

She sat on the window seat a long time just basking in the loveliness of the garden. It was a little world all of its own. It was such a beautiful place. Even though time would be short, being here with Dan would be a delight.

She arranged her things in the tiny bath and hung her dress and other things that she had brought for the short weekend. I'll read for a while she thought, as she reached for her constant companion, a book.

Comfortable in a large chair, she read for a long time and then she closed her eyes and drifted off for a quick nap.

She was awakened by a quiet knock on her door. She immediately became alert. It must be Dan, she thought as she got up to answer the knock. She turned the door knob a bit and she heard, "Chris it's me."

She unhitched the chain and promptly opened the door. Dressed in casual clothes and looking rugged, Dan stepped inside, dropped his bags and took her in his arms, holding her close. "I could hardly wait to get here. It seems like forever since I've seen you."

"Me too." She shook her head in agreement and smiled warmly.

She fell in his arms and he kissed her long and tenderly.

"Any problems getting here," he said.

"No, it was a nice drive. How was your day?"

"My day went well although I was very busy. Been here long?"

"Little over an hour. Just enough time to get settled and read and I closed my eyes. Also I enjoyed the view. Come and look," she said as she took his hand and led him to the window. "I don't think you can see this from your room. It's eleven."

"Eleven," he said abruptly. "You reserved two different rooms. I'm not staying with you, but I'm going to marry you," he stated emphatically.

His words had caused her to be mute. She was immediately concerned. They seem to be in the midst of a misunderstanding.

"Dan, I don't believe you have asked me to marry you. You have made statements to that end, but . . . and further more I haven't said yes."

He was rather startled and gazed out the window and seemingly lost for words.

Then warmly he looked directly into her sparkling brown eyes and said, "I love you Christina and people in love are together. And that is what I want, to be with you. I want to make love to you now, this night and every night for the rest of our lives. I want to show you love. I want you to know every part of me and I you. And now you tell me room eleven. I'll be patient."

With that he said, "You made dinner reservations for seven."

"Yes, seven," she could not say more.

He glanced at his watch. "It's six now and I'll get my key, get dressed and call for you at seven," he smiled but it was a bit forced.

He turned and left her room. She closed the door and wondered if the whole evening would be spoiled. I must truly and completely be sure before I can make love to him, she thought. An event in the past had treated her so ruthlessly she wondered if love would even happen for her again.

Christina treated herself to a refreshing shower, hoping to wash away the upset that had just occurred. Afterward she brushed her soft brown hair many times. After relaxing a few moments, she put on her dress. She had brought her little black summer dress for the evening. The short sleeves and rounded neckline added to her own natural beauty. It followed the outline of her perfectly shaped body. A dress she also felt comfortable wearing, but as she gazed in the mirror, she noticed she lacked the radiance that love brings to a person.

She tried hard not to think of the present sensitive issue. She wanted everything to be pleasant as it had been before. She would do her part to mend the hurt feelings and yet she must abide by her own delicate wishes.

It was seven and there was a light knock on her door. She let Dan in and he presented a big and wonderful smile.

"I've called for my lady and she looks lovely," he said.

"The little black dress is always a favorite of mine."

His words immediately put Christina at ease.

"You look pretty handsome yourself," she returned the compliment.

"I apologize for last hour and I understand. I want this to be a wonderful time, it is such a short one."

He leaned forward and kissed her lightly on the cheek.

"Me too," she said. "One more thing, I bought a new pair of earrings in the village and I want to put them on."

"Let me do it," he said softly.

A little surprised she said, "You know how?"

"I know how."

Very easily he slipped the earrings into her tiny little earlobes. His hands rubbed across her neck and sent waves of warm all through her body.

"All done." He looked at each one. "I like them very much . . . shall we go."

He took her hand and they went down stairs to the lounge and were seated in the dining room.

"This is a beautiful place," Christina said as she started the conversation. "I've only seen it from the outside."

"I was here at that mini convention I mentioned before. We stayed overnight. I thought it was pretty nice. Just close enough from the big city that it can do well as an inn."

"I want to tell you about your interview that you know everything about already."

"Oh yeah. How did I do?"

"Papa and I watched and we both thought it was very nice. Everything was smooth and we thought you covered some good points. It was a good balanced discussion about where and why the photos were taken. Overall excellent."

"I'm glad to hear that because it felt okay as we were taping it. I really enjoyed doing it."

"Also I was reading a lot of the text without looking too much at the photos and you're a really good writer. Have you ever thought about writing . . . maybe a novel? Your descriptions are beautiful, now just add conversation."

"Yeah, I haven't had time to really work at something like that. But I have thought about it."

"It was good that you mentioned that you lived here for a while."

"It probably perked up some ears. I remember that kid. We didn't get involved in much but we did get acquainted with a few people at church."

They talked on about everything, Christina shopping, Dan's work schedule and the week that had just passed. He told her in a week he was going to Detroit, but he wasn't sure how long, probably a week or ten days.

"What will you be doing? "

"Another symphony booklet. They saw the one we did and liked it and asked us to do theirs. They have the interviews all lined up. Rehearsals and even a formal party, but I'll be there working. I enjoy filming the interviews but they have packed them so close together. But I like doing these. The musicians are so intense and I try to capture that. And you think you have done that but it has to translate to the one that is viewing the photo."

"I believe you have accomplished that."

"I suppose, but let's think about how we can get intense," and he smiled and she knew that he was being a little playful.

The more they talked the happier they seemed to be.

Their carafe of wine gone, all the food including dessert and the candle low, they decided to enjoy the gardens.

They walked hand in hand along the path to the pond. It was the best of summer evenings. A soft breeze gently moved the leaves in a whisper. The large tree branches hung low, enclosing them from the outside world. They sat down on a park bench and he put his arm around her and she snuggled close. They sat there just listening to the softness of summer gently passing by. The sun was setting behind the tall trees and dusk was coming fast. He easily turned her face and he kissed her. They sat just being together as the darkness was slowly moving in.

"Let's walk back," Dan suggested.

She took his hand and they strolled back among the trees and branches.

"I noticed the outdoor dance floor over there. Shall we go," Dan asked. "We could work off some of our dinner." He also thought it would fall naturally to hold her close.

"Oh yeah," she replied as she looked that way.

The dance floor partially under the tree and partially under the sky was surrounded with gaslights. As the tiny flame flickered softly, Christina and Dan danced gracefully in each other's arms. "We're good together," she said.

"We are and would you look at that moon on the horizon. I don't think I've ever seen it so bright, a dusty orange and look how big!"

They stopped, their arms around each other, and gazed at this phenomenon of beauty.

"It couldn't be more beautiful and it is just for us," Chris said as she looked lovingly at Dan.

"It's really romantic and we're right here in the middle of it.

"I was thinking that too," she said quietly.

The night filled with music they turned and reached for each other, but they were beyond dancing. Her head on his shoulder and his face nestled in her soft brown hair they moved ever so slowly. He stopped and pulled her closer and she responded to feel the warmth that was his. The world of other things was far away.

He whispered, "You fit so nicely in my arms. You fit so nicely in my heart."

The soft music touched their emotions as only music can. They let this surround them and pull them to each other. Music will guide love to the heart and it's for the soul in love.

He whispered again, "When I'm with you it gets me away from the world. I forget there is sadness. You help me to be happy and most of all you have shown me love."

They shared their emotions under the twinkling stars, each twinkle a note of music from the heavens.

Softly, "We can never capture these moments again. I want you to feel them—completely. They are ours for our memory book."

She accepted his beautiful soft words and they touched her heart. She could feel that he desired more than words. Although she felt he was sincere, she needed total assurance before giving herself completely. There was a silence in her heart but Dan had touched a chord that she liked. She felt she could go forward but not too fast.

With their eyes closed, they did not notice that darkness had surrounded them.

Then Dan whispered, "Want to go in. My room has a lounge area and we can snuggle and have tea or coffee. And I'll tell you all about the antique car show," he said jokingly.

Dan thought I can hardly contain myself I love her so much, although I will not be aggressive. I don't want to destroy what we have between us. To wait a few days, a few weeks is a small trade–off for a lifetime with her.

Chris too liked the feeling that Dan gave her. And she questioned, was this the emotion that I like or is it Dan or are they one.

They went in and as they passed the desk Dan ordered tea to be brought to his room.

They relaxed on the couch with their tea and television. They snuggled so very close.

"It's nice being here with you," she said warmly.

"Yes it's nice to relax after a busy day and special to have you here. Tomorrow I'll have to relax alone."

Dan was a little surprised, but oh so happy to hear her say those words. But he knew the time was not right for any further advances, but with little encouragement he felt he could open her heart to him.

After a while, he said, "I have to leave early so I'll get you to your room and we can get a good night's sleep. I'll stop by in the morning, it will be early. I'll knock and if you are awake." With that he walked with her to her room.

"I can take those earrings off for you if you would like," he said once inside.

She whisked her hair back and held her head as he did the task. Then he kissed each ear lightly.

Christina thought, oh my, what one tiny little bit of affections can do to the body. With that he simply said goodnight and kissed her lightly on the cheek. He knew if he kissed her once more it might be . . .

♥

Dan woke early and quickly dressed. It would be too early to get any breakfast at the inn, so he thought he would pick up something along the way to the stadium. I must see if she is awake, to be so close and not see her even for just a moment.

Bag in hand he stopped and knocked lightly on Christina's door. He thought he heard a slight noise. Chain secured she peeked out.

He asked, "May I come in just for a moment?"

"You probably don't want to see me so early," she said.

"Oh yes I do," he said emphatically.

"Let me unhitch this."

He stepped inside, "Did you sleep well?" he asked as he took her hand.

"I did," she replied. "Did you?" As those words came out she realized he might tell her.

"It could have been better. This conversation is for another day," he smiled. "I have only a moment.

It's like getting to work on time. My schedule is very full for the next two weeks. I have to go to Detroit on the twenty–eighth and won't be back until after Labor Day. The Friday before I go is free. I can come out for the day."

"I believe that's okay."

"Then I have a very full week. After that we can get together. How about the next weekend? The middle of October I have to go to London for no more than a month. We'll squeeze in time together amidst all this chaos. After London I will plan not to be so busy on weekends. Speaking of a squeeze, I need a morning hug."

She smiled and stepped to him and they held each other in a long embrace. Willingly she was in his arms. A thin robe and nighty did not leave much to Dan's imagination. Oh my god, he thought and I have to go away. Why didn't this happen last night?

"Bye sweetie. Next time will not come fast enough."

"I've loved being with you and looking forward to next time too," she said softly while looking into his big dark eyes.

He was on his way to the stadium and Christina left later in the morning for home.

CHAPTER EIGHT

♥

The days until school starting and Christmas were getting closer and there was much work to be done. Especially Christmas, there are several small toys to be finished. She had completed two little pinafores and there were two more to be made. She hoped they would fit because little girls grow fast. And they all had to be alike or similar. She bought the little boys something special or different, but made gifts for all. She tried hard to please each one and considered their likes and dislikes. She knew the children well because they visited them often and she talked to them frequently on the phone. She was a caring aunt.

It was her only way of enjoying the world of very young children. With Brian gone hopes for children of her own had faded, so she devoted the time to her nieces and nephews.

She had taken over her mother's sewing room and making presents was a diversion from school curriculum. She felt she had not mastered the art of sewing yet, but she was working very hard to learn this craft.

Since Dan so suddenly had entered her life she hadn't finished preparing for the beginning of this school year. Also she had missed some of the non–mandatory meetings on Friday scheduled in August. This was not like Christina. Most of her colleagues knew that she was home this month and were wondering why she had not been at the meetings. It created a buzz, why? But the meetings were not mandatory so nothing much was made of it. She was very busy preparing at home.

She had not told anyone about her new friend Dan, except Jan, who was still at her home in Arizona. They had called and written all summer and she was due back soon for the opening of classes in September.

♥

Friday before leaving for Detroit on Saturday, Dan came out and they spent the day together. He arrived early and Christina and the dogs walked out to the car to meet him.

He kissed her lightly, "This is a perfect day for just about anything. What have you planned?"

"Have you had breakfast?"

"Yes but a coffee would be nice and you can tell me what we're going to do."

"I haven't planned much. I thought I would give you a choice. We can always go to the gallery or museum, shop. Just stay around here. We can play pool downstairs, listen to music in the library, walk to the pond."

"If we hurry we can do all that. Let's stay here. It's a wonderful break from the city. I'd especially like a walk to the pond."

"Bring your camera, there is nearly always some wildlife there."

"I'm ready. I'll get my camera."

And they were off for the long walk to the pond.

"It's down back of the barn and through the woods. There is a path, not quite as worn as in the past. There are many springs around here that feed it."

"Did you swim here?"

"Off limits unless supervised. Papa was strict about that. The boys could get a little, shall we say active. Although papa built a dock and they had a couple canoes. I know they swam down there when papa wasn't looking. They kept it from me too because they were afraid I would tell. We have to go slow now and quietly, so if there is anything here we'll see it."

And there was. "Look," and Chris pointed, "a heron over there and a few ducks. Not too much now but later the Canadian geese will be flying and then there is usually quite a few."

They proceeded quietly and sat down on an old bench that had been placed there years before.

119

"It's really big and so peaceful. I bet it is really beautiful in the fall."

"Some years the beauty takes your breath away. I have some pictures of past years and I'll show you sometime."

"I bet you ice skated too."

"We did. That was a big thing. Papa had my brothers keep a record of the temperature and how many days below freezing. When it reached a certain point Papa would have the ice tested. Then we could skate. We're far enough north that we did a lot, especially January and February. We would have friends over. Papa would build a fire. Roast marshmallows. Sometime other parents would come too and keep mother and Papa company.

While snuggling close to Dan, Christina told him more about the farm and how the city had grown closer.

"There is about two hundred acres going south and Papa leases it out. He uses the money for the upkeep of the house. It can be costly when you need something big, like a roof. Although papa usually gets discounts because of his business. His firm did lots of work for different contractors."

Dan took pictures and they enjoyed the quiet of this isolated area.

"I would like to take some macro pictures. I saw mushrooms on the logs, interesting wood formations. You can do a lot with the small version."

"Anytime, things are always changing."

With his arm around her he pulled her close and said, "Here we are among nature again. I hold you close to keep you warm and I hold you close because I love you."

Chris turned and looked into his eyes and ran her finger tips across his beautiful mouth and he kissed her. "You know I want to do more than kiss your lips."

A shy and knowing smile crossed her face and she thought, I do too but I need time.

They walked back to the house and it was about noon. Chris fixed a quick lunch.

In the afternoon they relaxed in the library and listened to music and also a few games of pool in the rec room in the cellar.

After a while Dan asked her, "Would you like to go to the Carriage House for an early dinner. I'd like to get back to the city so I can get a good night's sleep. It is a very early flight. Short but early and the only flight over there tomorrow."

"If we have enough time."

"I think so. I brought some clean clothes. If I could freshen up."

"Get your things and I'll show you where and I can do the same."

Dan got his things from his car and Christina took him to the guest room and said, "You can take a shower if you would like and I'll meet you in the library in an half hour."

"Good timing but first let me hold you close." She did and they were so close they could feel every curve of each other's body.

"The library," she said.

He whispered, "You feel so wonderful."

Half an hour they were both in the library and Chris ask him, "Would you rather go somewhere closer?"

"Maybe that would be better. Can you suggest?"

"There is a nice grill on the way to the city."

"You will have to tell me how to get there."

In the car Chris guided and they were soon there.

"This is a nice place," he said as he looked around.

"Yes, me, Papa and Ellen come over sometimes."

They chose from the menu and with conversation and laughs, it was a quick but delightful time.

They drove home and Dan stopped his car and he moved over near her.

"I know we're going to be extremely busy, they have already warned us, but I'll call as soon as I get there and give you a phone number. I'm going to miss you."

He touched her face lightly and drew her near. He kissed her warmly and then more passionately and she responded with her arms around him.

He thought this is so hard when you love someone so much and she doesn't quite have the same feeling, and would she ever.

"As far as I know I should be home by Tuesday or Wednesday. Again I accepted this assignment before I met you. If only I had known. But I love you so much."

"Dan," and she paused, "everything will work out. It has to be naturally."

"I know," he said softly. "I have to go now, as I mentioned, it's an early flight."

"Be safe. I want you back," she said as she held his face in both of her hands.

Dan walked to the door with her and said, "I'll say goodnight here."

There embrace was gentle but held much passion.

She stood on the porch as he walked away. He turned as he reached his car and waved. She waved and threw him a kiss.

He was gone and as ever Christina watched from the big window, with her faithful companions at her side.

♥

Saturday midday Dan called Christina, "We got here and I'm at the hotel." And he gave her the phone number.

"My instructions were waiting."

"When do you start?"

"Tomorrow at eight. They said plan for all day. This afternoon I am going over what we will be doing and do some creative planning and then take a nap. Oh how I wish you were here."

Christina did not know what to say. There was silence.

"I'll call you tonight and we can talk."

"Good, you can tell me about your creative thoughts."

"My creative thoughts are about you dear heart and they are very sincere. I'll call you after I have something to eat, after a while. Bye love."

"I'll be here. Bye also."

Later that evening Dan did call and they talked for a long time.

♥

With Dan gone until after Labor Day she would be able to finish preparing for the opening of school and also make plans for the next several months. Christina had her books and papers all spread out on the dining table and there she was working Wednesday evening when the phone rang. Of course she thought it was Dan. Excited, she answered to find it was Jan. She had returned early from her home out west.

Christina and Jan had much in common and were ready to start their third year as friends as well as colleagues. Since Brian was no longer in Christina's life, she and Jan spent much time together, preparing for their classes and going places together. They both cared for each other and their friendship was very strong.

"Hi Jan," Chris exclaimed. "You're back. I didn't expect you for a few more days."

"Mom and Dad were leaving so rather than spend a few days alone, I would just get back here and get settled."

"I'm glad, when can we get together," Chris asked.

"Well I do have a suggestion, if you don't have any plans, I was wondering if you would like to go to the Shire for the weekend and catch a couple plays before school starts."

"Oh yes, that's a great idea and I don't have any plans. My new friend Dan, that I wrote you about is away until next week, Tuesday I think. I can't wait to tell you more about him."

"Want to go Saturday morning and we can come back Tuesday morning early?"

"That sounds good. Come on out and we can leave from here since it is closer. Do you want me to call for reservations, same place?" Chris asked.

Jan replied in the affirmative and they continued to talk and make a few necessary arrangements.

The next day Chris worked on her school plans, worked around the house and made phone calls. She wanted to tell Dan that she and Jan were going to the Shire but he had not called again. If he doesn't, I will call Friday evening and leave a message. And when we get together next time I will tell him all about it. Or if he calls papa can tell him where I went. Anyway we'll be back before he is. Friday late Dan had not called so she called the hotel and left a message for him.

♥

Jan and Christina had visited the Shire on the Lake several times. It was a quaint little village with a big role in theatre. It also had boutiques and shops that made shopping an event rather than a routine stop.

Last year they met an interesting man and Christina had hoped that something special would happen again this year.

She and Jan had stopped at the bookstore on Main Street, where Jan was looking for a book about the Caesars. After inquiring at the information desk, they were directed to the shelf that held several. As they looked through the books, they talked about seeing *Caesar and Cleopatra* the next evening. It was then that a distinguished gentleman standing nearby overheard them talking and joined the conversation. After several minutes of exchanging ideas on the topic they revealed their respective professions, two English teachers and one English professor turned actor. The gentleman was playing Caesar in the play they were to see the next evening. It was then he asked them to join him for dinner that evening at the Windsor Room.

The next evening they attended the performance. Having met Herbert Callaghan made it even more delightful. It was the highlight of their visit and they talked about it for quite some time.

Christina was so glad Jan was back and their going to the Shire would be a good way to start the school year. Jan could tell her all about her summer in Arizona and Christina could tell her about her new friend Dan.

♥

Dan was miles away but his heart was near Christina.

She had so completely and so quickly captured his heart. Each time he had been with her and each time he had talked on the phone he knew he was falling more in love. Her beauty was such a small part of why he loved her. Her warm soft smile and calm voice and gentle ways all living together in this delicate energetic body. And yes those sexy eyes of brown that left an imprint on your soul. They stayed with you long after she was gone. Her maturity also impressed him. She seemed at ease with life's problems and able to cope with a wide variety of incidents. With his varied work schedule, he needed someone that would be able to accept his irregular life style. Christina seemed perfect in every way.

It also pleased Dan that their professions were in the artistic field. They could even work together. She could edit his writing or do the writing for any books that he might do in the future. She could certainly advise him on literary topics. They were intellectually compatible and together they could be a team, each offering a portion of the humanities. It couldn't have been any better if it had been planned, he thought. But Dan was puzzled why she had not been swept away by someone else. She was desirable in every way. Why was she hiding away on her father's farm? Could there be someone else?

She was warm, responsive and yet sometimes, something would take her away. She would interrupt the present and create a distance between the now and another time. She would look far away and her eyes would become empty and lifeless. The beautiful expression on her face would grow dull and blank. Her body would become still and it seemed she would slip into another time. The contrast of emotions from her spirited personality to one of languor was very evident. This happened too frequently to be idle thoughts or momentary distractions. These actions of the human spirit in a flash of time would probably not be noticed by many. But Dan had been trained to observe and capture silent emotions. They spoke loud and were very noticeable to him. He never interrupted or asked her what she was thinking about. They seemed to be too definite or private. He never intruded, but only waited for her return. He simply pretended not to notice.

Dan felt certain that all the problems, if there were any, would resolve themselves. Time takes care of many things and to this he would add his love.

♥

Work in Detroit had been very hectic, they started early and stayed late. They all wanted to be done before the Labor Day weekend. And that they did.

Dan arrived home very late Saturday night. With little sleep, Sunday morning he packed clean clothes and drove out to Christina's city and checked in at the hotel. He wanted to surprise her. He did not wait long to call her. Her father answered the phone and when Dan asked for her, Papa Zeller promptly said she is away for the weekend with Dan and would not be back until Tuesday morning. Before either could say more, Dan said thank you and hung up.

Totally startled, away with Dan. No! No! She's not. I'm here, he thought. What's going on? Did she tell her father she was away with me? Where? Is there another Dan in her life? I can't call back. If there is another person in her life, I want to hear it from her, not her father.

Very puzzled, why had she not mentioned that she was going to be away for the weekend? He immediately thought, I guess I'm the one that got the surprise!

It was Sunday and Christina would not be back until Tuesday, I can't stay here he said to himself. Anyway I have to check in with Kate Tuesday morning. I'll drive up and see mom and dad. They are always glad to see me. He called his mother and yes they would be home and your brother will be here.

As he drove to his parents' home, thousands of serious thoughts went through his mind. It can't be over, it's hardly begun. I love her so much, this can't be the end. Is there someone else? Why is she distant at times? Have I been taking this friendship too fast? One question begets another. The more he thought about the situation the more distraught he became. I hope love hasn't made me foolish. Why have I been so naïve?

Dan also thought of the tender moments and how he had held her so close and how she responded so willingly. It just can't end this way.

He spent Sunday at his parents' home. Everyone being there was a nice surprise for all of them. Dan thought only one thing would make it better, had Christina been there too. He so much wanted her to complete his family. But he didn't even know where she was or who she was with.

He told the family what had happened and that he was totally bewildered. They all assured him that it was just a misunderstanding and Dan certainly hoped they were right. But in his own mind there was fear, because he had a big picture of their time together and some of it had been more than wonderful but other times distant.

Monday afternoon he went back to the city and did just what he always did before he met Christina. Bookstores, eating alone, a long walk, reading and some writing. Maybe she is trying to tell me something with her absence of words. I'll call her Tuesday evening when I have time to talk. That is all I can do.

♥

Christina and Jan decided to come home Monday evening after the afternoon play instead of Tuesday. They arrived home tired but joyful about their good time. They had a pleasant three days visiting art shops, seeing plays and they talked, talked and talked. There was much to catch up on. Their summer was coming to an end and it had been good for both of them.

In the past, summers had always been extra special for Christina because as they got older she and Brian had been inseparable. As they came to realize they were soul mates and wanted to be married someday, there was hardly a moment when they were apart. They rode, they picnicked, they read, they ate together and yes they argued about things only to make up.

The last two summers had been difficult and lonely for Christina. Late this summer Dan came into her life and things moved all too quickly to be real. She still was not sure of Dan's sincerity and she was not over losing Brian. An emotional combination she was not sure how to handle. But now all the pleasantries of this summer were over and she would finish preparing for school and relax these few days before it would begin.

Her arrival home had been greeted exuberantly by her father and the dogs.

After telling him all about the nice things, the plays, the shopping, she seemed to settle in.

"Honey, you had three phone calls. No one left a name, but I'm sure one was Dan and I told him you had gone to the Shire with Jan."

She was excited to hear that one call was from Dan.

"When did he call?"

"I think it was him that called Sunday morning. He quickly said thank you and hung up."

"He was on a busy and tight schedule. That's strange, in the message I left I told him we would be back Tuesday morning, yet he called Sunday. He probably was in a hurry. I think he is supposed to come home tomorrow."

Papa also told her that he had finalized his plans to go to San Francisco next Thursday morning. He continued by saying Ellen would take him to the airport since she would be in school that day.

♥

The next day Christina prepared for the opening of school and caught up on her household duties.

In the evening she prepared a small dinner for herself and her father. When dinner was over she said, "I'm going to call Dan, he might be home."

He was and promptly answered the phone. She thought he sounded a bit distant, but maybe he just got home and was probably tired.

She opened the conversation with friendly words. All too soon she realized she was carrying the conversation alone. Dan was responding with a yes or no. Realizing his responses were short, she abruptly asks, "Dan I know you're probably tired and when did you get home?"

He replied with restraint. "I was just wondering why you did not tell me you were going away for the weekend. And your father said with Dan—not this Dan! Is there another gentleman in your life? I'm very puzzled. We finished filming early and I got home late Saturday and I came out and was going to surprise you, but I was the one that got surprised." He continued talking and his voice got more agitated.

Christina totally baffled and could hear the distress in his voice and could not imagine what he was talking about

"I'm not sure if I understand you but it sounds like you are wondering why I didn't tell you I was going away and with whom."

"Yes Chris, I'm asking. Is there someone else in your life?"

"No! No! My dear, I went with my friend Jan. Papa said I went with Dan. No! No! He must have been excited and twisted names, they do sound alike. Did you talk to him?"

"No, I was too surprised and distressed to hear unwanted news. If there's someone else in your life, I wanted to hear it from you."

"Jan came back a few days early and we went to the Shire. We had been there several times. And since you would not be back until Tuesday, you would never miss me and anyway I left a message at the hotel telling you that we were going. Did you get it?"

"No, I didn't get any message," he replied.

"Oh no! Awful! You would have understood everything. I'm so sorry, I didn't mean to upset you or keep anything from you. Oh Dan! You're the only guy in my life."

"I did feel awful and went up to Mom's and came home Monday. I just hung around the city wondering where you were and what you were doing. Christina, I love you so much. I have never really loved anyone before and I can't imagine losing you."

As he talked he slowly calmed down and became more relaxed. "When can I see you? Next Saturday and Sunday I have free. If you don't have plans I would like very much to come out and we can do something."

"I'm free, and would love to have you come out. Things are okay," she asked

"Yes, things are okay," he responded gently. "I'll be in touch before then. Good luck starting school."

"Thank you. It's going to be a good year."

Warm and loving goodbyes were exchanged and with their misunderstanding explained, they both felt better.

CHAPTER NINE

♥

The weather had grown slightly cool with the passing of summer. The warm evenings that had been full of sounds were being replaced by the cool stillness of the coming fall. The sunsets were earlier and sunrises later. Red, oranges and gold were beginning to replace the greens of summer. Summer was slipping away. The days had passed quickly.

With school starting, it was always a busy time. Meeting new students was always a challenge. Introducing them to writing and literature of the ages and hope to share the knowledge of this beauty as well as inspiring them, was Christina's main goal.

Also papa would leave for a two week visit to San Francisco with son John and his wife Rachel and their girls. They wanted him to come out now because they have plans to come home for Christmas.

Dan would be here for the weekend. Christina was thinking of things they could do. There was much to choose from and they both liked the same things. Deciding would be easy. Papa being away she could have a candle light dinner at home. Something she had not been able to do and that she planned.

♥

Saturday morning Christina was getting ready for the two days with Dan. It was just ten o'clock when the dogs announced his arrival. She went out to meet him and as usual he kissed her long, but lightly, as a greeting.

"Are we okay?" He first asked.

Her loving reply, "Yes, we're okay."

After a brief hello to Daisy and Henry, they all went into the house Beautiful music was all around.

He stopped and listened for a moment. "Mahler?" he questioned.

"Yes, his fifth, a favorite of mine," she answered.

"I like most of his compositions. His music is unpredictable and refreshing as well as melodic. I did a study of Mahler in college. Although I don't play an instrument, I am a music lover. I took several music classes in college after I decided to do photography because I realized it creates an emotion. So when I can I have music playing when I'm photographing. It certainly sets a mood and nearly always is reflected in an expression or a movement."

"Me too, music and words such beauty in both," she said as she took his hand and asked. "Mid–morning coffee."

"Yes, before that I'll say a hello to your father."

"He's gone," she replied and before she could continue they started for the kitchen and the conversation had changed. She did not say where.

They settled at the kitchen table and she asked, "How was your drive?"

"Uneventful but nice. Early enough that there wasn't much traffic. Saturday morning in the big city everyone sleeps until noon," he added. "But I had a mission, to be with you," he said as he reached for her hand.

She smiled softly. With coffee, rolls and fruit enjoyed she said, "Come into the library and I'll show you my new painting. Two pictures I found and am kind of putting them together. I probably should be working on Christmas presents, but I was inspired to paint. It won't take too long."

They made their way to the library and she explained what she was trying to capture and how it was progressing.

Dan listened attentively, "It's beautiful and I want to see all of your other works. We'll have time."

"Tomorrow, I have them all in my brother Jim's bedroom. It has the most space. Papa is helping me choose for the gallery show, The Nature Gallery. Maybe you would make some suggestions too. They want ten."

"I'd love to. A show of your own, that is great. How did they find out about your talent?"

"The art teacher at school. We had our faculty Christmas party out here last year and the art teacher saw them and he ask me, then he went to make arrangements for a show. I think they are trying to schedule it for late winter. But today I thought we'd see some real professional stuff. And at the art museum at three o'clock there is an organ recital. Have you heard about the little Baroque pipe organ from Italy?"

"I did," he exclaimed. "Mom sent me a clipping from the paper, and yes I would like to hear it."

"They last about forty–five minutes. The courtyard is such a perfect place, it's open, bright. Papa and I went to hear it soon after it was installed. It has a beautiful sound. So clear and mellow."

"Can I go like this, although I brought different clothes for dinner tonight?"

"Fine for the museum," as she looked him up and down. "You don't have to dress for dinner tonight. I'm going to fix a candlelight dinner here at the big table, just for the two of us. Or we can fix it together."

"Splendid," he said, "I'll do what I can, but I have no culinary skills."

"That's okay, we'll just grill steaks and a few little things to go with it," she replied.

"That will be perfect."

"If you have had enough to eat, we can be off to the city."

"I have. Let's be on our way."

♥

As they drove to the city Dan asked, "Do you paint outside? Fall is such a colorful time of the year."

"Not too much. I work from pictures that I have taken or just look out one of the windows and then I add my own touch." She laughed a little. "I find painting very satisfying but it gets neglected at times. I felt enriched that I developed my skills in school. I also took some art history classes. I enjoyed most of my art classes, but literature just simply won out."

"When did you decide you wanted literature as your major," he asked.

"Seriously, when I first went to high school. My mother was my mentor. She was an English teacher too, although she never insisted, but she was there when I decided. She would read the assignments with me and explain, tell me about the authors, when they were written and how their writings applied to their culture or the times. We would sit at the big dining room table, read and discuss. I was actually over–prepared," and she laughed a little.

"You were probably the best informed person in class," Dan interjected.

"Almost," she added. "It was those evenings spent with my mother that are such wonderful memories. I owe so much to her."

What Christina failed to add, that Brian was almost always there too. The four years of high school they took the same classes with few exceptions. Brian took a few more math classes. So in the literature classes it was the battle between Christina and Brian who could offer the most information about the assignment for the day. Sometimes they even dominated the class.

Brian thought it was absolutely wonderful that Christina's mother would sit with them in the evening and share her time and knowledge. Brian did not have that attention from his own mother. She was a good mother and he loved her but she had to work many hours to support her small family. So Christina shared her mother with him. Of course he too liked being with Christina. And when the evening was over usually Papa would drive him home.

"Not having any children younger than you was also an advantage," Dan added.

"Oh yes, she did a lot with me that she didn't do with the boys. They had sports. Jim and Dave were in the band. Papa did a lot of tutoring with my brothers or just a little help with their math. One or both of my parents and of course me, always went to their events."

"You have your masters. Did you think about getting your doctorate?"

"Yes I have, but later. I thought I would teach a few years. Keep studying, reading and let things fall into place. After that teach in a college somewhere. Just thoughts."

"So you want to stay in teaching."

"Yes, but if I can do something with literature, then I would consider. Literature is like looking into the soul. It encompasses all that we are as human beings. It speaks, it describes emotions for us when we can't. It speaks through symbolisms. It is also a teaching tool. Analyzing. Structure. I've been going on too long."

"Let's talk about your profession. You capture moments in time that will never occur again." She continued, "That is quite a statement and then you add the text that creates another emotion and you have a beautiful piece of work. As your books are."

"Thank you. Almost always I have to travel, long or short distances to get to my subject, which can be good. Travel is an added perk."

"I travel vicariously when I read, this is where the imagination kicks in. You're free to go all over the place," she added and then laughed.

"Don't we have the most wonderful careers?" he said joyfully as he reached for her hand.

They arrived at the museum so this delightful conversation had to end at least for now. They would now delve into the world of the artist and musician.

They began with the first room of modern paintings and then on to the sculptures.

"We have a great selection of sculptures in studio, not originals of course, and I try to match one with a subject that I am photographing."

"That sounds like a labor of love."

"It is, that and music. Do you have a favorite period of time?"

"Yes, I believe it would be Impressionism."

"And . . ."

"Camille Pissarro. But it's so unfair to pick one."

"I like Impressionism because the whole spectrum can be defined in many different ways. Many other mediums of painting are precise, but not this one. Do you have one?"

"Not really, but then I have never studies any in depth. But I like some artist over others," he answered.

They continued discussing histories, resting in front of their favorites. Discussing why they were their favorite and not others. The background music added to the atmosphere of these artistic works.

"Chris I believe you said the recital was at three. It's getting close."

"Yes, let's go on up to the courtyard."

The organ had been brought from a small church in Italy, restored and placed here in the museum. The music students from the university gave recitals here every weekend.

"This is such a perfect spot for this instrument," he said as they walked into the big bright room. "The courtyard is so big and the organ is so small."

"But wait till you hear the sound. It's wonderful."

The young lady that was to play soon entered the room and announced her selections. Dan and Chris sat close as the music began and it knew no end around the large open courtyard. The clarity of the sound was unbelievable and they both were emotionally affected. Dan squeezed her hand and the artistic force flowed between them. Neither wanted this to end, but as many things, this did also.

♥

As they made their way to his car Dan said, "That was a real treat. It is a work of art even without the sound. Quite an addition to the museum and great for student to perform."

"You enjoyed see and hearing."

"Oh yes, you were right. What a sound."

As they drove home they were so engrossed in the beauty they had just seen and heard they hardly noticed that it had turned cooler and the sun had faded.

"Our sunny day is gone," Dan finally noticed.

"I hope it doesn't rain before we get our steaks grilled," she said.

When they reached home Dan helped Chris start the grill in the back yard. She put the potatoes in the oven and had already prepared the salad before Dan arrived.

"While the grill gets ready and the potatoes bake let's take the dogs for a little walk. They have been in the house all day and need to run. We can walk up to the top of the hill. There is a big path. They love running up there, carrying their sticks. Sometimes I ride my bike with them. I'll feed them when we get back. Their appetite will be good and they won't beg at the table."

"You let them do that," he asked.

"Oh, they do lots of things they're probably not supposed to, they're spoiled."

They walked to the top of the hill playing with the dogs throwing their ball and sticks and then they walked slowly back, hand in hand. Everyone relaxed on the back deck.

Christina brought a bottle of wine, two glasses and a plate to cheese and crackers. She also had a drink of water for the dogs. Dan poured the wine and after handing Christina her glass. He toasted, "To the love of my life and all that she is."

"Chris followed, "To a wonderful evening."

"Where is your papa? You mentioned earlier that he was gone but we went on to something else," he asked.

"Oh, he went to San Francisco Thursday to visit John and Rachel. They wanted him to come out now and he agreed because they planned to be here for Christmas. I believe all my brothers will be here. It is so wonderful having them all together and . . . oh! the house is so full! Just like the old days."

Soon the fire was ready to grill. Dan volunteered to do the job, while Christina got everything else ready.

Christina had prepared the table for the candlelight dinner before Dan arrived. The place setting was in the middle of the long dining table, across from each other. She used a light blue tablecloth that covered the small area in the middle. Her silver was a rose pattern and in the middle she placed one pink rose. It was the only one she could find in the garden. She had created an intimate setting in this long and spacious table.

Just as Dan got the steaks off the grill it started to lightly rain and thunder could be heard in the distance.

"I believe we are in for a little storm because Daisy is acting weird. She does that before a storm. And she won't leave your side. You will have to share me or she might even want to sit on your lap," she laughed as she informed him.

144

He laughed too, "She's not exactly a lap dog. But I'll be understanding."

Dinner was ready and Christina dimmed the lights and Dan helped her with her chair and then went around to the other side of the table and sat down across from her. She lit the candles in the center of the table. *Music in the Night* was her choice of background music. Soft strings and totally romantic.

Holding her hand, "You have made this evening absolutely wonderful. Your home is gracious and elegant, the music perfect, just like you. Your long table indicated once there were many here. It must have been a great time," Dan concluded.

"We had all sort of emotions, very sad but the happy were very happy," she said with her voice a little tight.

"I didn't mean to make you sad."

"Oh no, you didn't. There has been so much love generated here it counteracts any sadness."

"Chris darling, a young beautiful intelligent lady," he paused, "you need to be loved," and he looked into her soft eyes as he finished his loving words, "by me."

She smiled shyly, but she felt his expression was sincere and determined.

"Everything is so perfect but your loving Daisy is over here drooling on my knee. His words truly broke the moment of a romantic feeling.

They both laughed.

"She is afraid when it rains especially thunders and goes to someone for comfort. That shows she likes you."

Chris took Daisy and put her in the kitchen and put up the gate. Henry had been content and found comfort in one of his many beds.

Chris and Dan continued their dinner with much laughter and leaving the serious talk behind. In spite of the rain and thunder there was a genuine air of comfort between them.

Dan continued to talk about her home and family. "What was it like growing up with four brothers?"

"They're a little older and they did boy things and they had their friends. I had different interests. We all liked horses and we rode together. My mother and I did lots together. She taught me to sew a little. I had little girl friends."

"We're lucky to have such great parents," Dan added.

"Oh yes, my mother was a wonderful guide for us into young and adult life. Papa was strict with the boys but not so much with me."

Dan smiled as he continued to listen to his original question being answered.

"I was unexpected. I think they thought their family was complete after David arrived. Then I came along."

"How glad I am for that."

"My oldest brother John probably looked after me the most. The other boys thought I was just another kid around."

Christina then went into one of those silent moments when she seemed to be thinking of the past. What she was thinking and did not want to tell Dan that her young life from fourteen on had been dominated willingly by Brian. Those were long years and thousands of memories had been made only to be slashed in one brief moment.

She realized that she was thinking too much of the past and not being in the present with Dan. She tried to continue the conversation as if she had been totally aware of only the present.

"My brothers, all of them were very good to me. We did have our moments. David was four when I was born and Papa tells he didn't quite know how to handle having a new kid younger than he was. Tell me about your brother."

"He is six years older than me and growing up we didn't have the same interests. And now we have a great adult relationship, but we are very different. It was my sister that I was very close to. She was a year older than me and she died when she was ten. It was so sudden. I knew what death was but did not understand why. Today I guess I still don't. We were inseparable for all that time and one day she was gone. I couldn't stop crying. Mother tried so hard to comfort me. This happening in my young life brought us ever so close and we're still that way now."

Christina listened with empathy because she too knew grief. She thought, it is an ugly emotion and it grabs and crushes the heart.

Dan smiled as he recalled the fun times, "We played trucks together, we played dolls together and we rode our bikes together. We both went everywhere with mom."

"I can't imagine you playing with dolls."

"But I did, but I also had a favorite teddy bear and he is still in my bedroom at home."

He looked at Chris and noticed that her eyes were heavy with tears.

"Enough of this talk. We'll have a lifetime to get caught up on the past. I don't want to make this wonderful evening sad."

"But sharing is getting to know each other better. It is all of what we are," and she reached for his hand and gave an understanding gaze. "But now, how about dessert? I made a trifle."

"Now I know there is chemistry between us because trifle is one of my favorite desserts," Dan said as he came forth with a happy smile.

"I laid a fire in the fireplace and if you would please light it, we'll have our dessert in the library."

Dan started the fire and she arrived with the trifle.

Christina pulled the blinds on the big bay window to keep the stormy weather out and the warmth in. And there they enjoyed their trifle and then snuggled on the couch while sipping tea.

"Speaking of your elegant home, this is quite a library, books as well as the woodwork," he said. "A small table for dessert, big chairs for reading. It is a beautiful room."

"I love it too. My grandfather commissioned the mantel from a local carver. The same person that did the mantle at Bellamy House. The library table was my grandmother's and the old bookcase too. And the books my mother started when papa brought her here as his bride."

"I don't remember your mother. I probably didn't see her the day I was here. We didn't come in your house, but we did get out of the car as we waited for Bill to get whatever it was. Your father came out and we all were introduced. How I came to notice you, was, you and two big, really big dogs came out on your front porch and one barked and got our attention. Then there was this young girl with braids and she ran off with her dogs. I just can't believe all this," he said as he shook his head.

"Me and my dogs. Chloe and Sable and they were big."

"The more I think about this, I remember, our schools were having a debate. We did this every year. Your brother's coach drove out here for something and he asked a couple of us from Saint Francis to ride along. Probably to get to know each other. See if Bill remembers it that way."

"What was your debate about?" Chris asked.

"I don't remember, I did several and not sure about this one."

"After mother starting having us kids she never taught formally. Her teaching took on a new dimension. Since I have been big enough I have been buying and adding books to it. Her love of words. That's why papa spends so much time here, he feels close to her."

"Your home has been in your family a long time?"

"Yes, a long time. My grandfather purchased the house and land when he was young. It was far from the city then, but now it is closer, especially the house. When my grandfather passed it became my father's. When we kids started coming, he added baths and bedrooms, expanded the kitchen, made the cellar larger. Being an architect he knew how and

149

where to expand. It grew as we grew. Now it's nearly empty. Papa and I keep it going."

This had become a very wonderful evening and Christina wanted to think only of being with Dan. But their talking about her home and family, she couldn't help thinking that she and Brian had planned to live here and raise their children here, as her parents before. But for now she thought she would live here with her father and then probably alone.

Dan pulled her close and she forgot those thoughts as she snuggled warmly in his arms. It seemed there was complete surrender. The warmth of their bodies came together and drew each other near. The music gave way to silence and a hush fell over the room. Their soft words to each other became few. Gradually those few words became still. The silent moments were longer and longer. As the candlelight went out and the fire burned slowly keeping pace with the evening, Chris and Dan fell near asleep in each other's arms.

The world outside had become a little more stormy and the rain was quite heavy.

Dan was the first to speak, "Oh I believe we had a quick nap. The second time, remember at the creek side, the first. It is still raining out, sounds rather hard. It's late and I had better go."

"Did you make reservations in town?"

"No I came directly here. I thought I wouldn't have a problem getting a room at the Windham."

"You can't go out in this storm!" she said emphatically.

He slowly glanced at her, "Well . . . ."

Her reply seemed like hours to Dan but it was only seconds when she answered. "We have four extra bedrooms, the boys and two, as you know, have been turned into guest rooms. I'll offer you one of them—no charge." She giggled a little.

Dan wanted to answer quickly but he waited, "I accept your generous offer," and looking at her with a raised brow.

"So your clothes are in your car?"

"They are. I can get them but I'll probably get soaked."

They rose from their contentment and moved around a little. "This rain probably won't let up for a while. I'll be brave and go to the car now."

"Papa has the back garage all cleaned out and you can put your car in there. Just drive around to the back and I'll go through the kitchen and open the door for you."

As Dan ran to his car he managed to get very wet. He drove to the back garage where Christina was waiting.

Inside she said, "Let's get you settled, you are really wet and you can put on your robe."

Shyly he looked at her and then said, "No robe."

"Well then your pajamas."

Silly girl he thought, "No pajamas."

Christina was lost for words, "Well I'll find you something."

In one of the back closets she found a robe that would do for now. He took off his shirt and she dried off his back and he put on the robe. Christina sparkled at his handsome physique although she did not want it to be obvious.

Oh how I would love to sleep with her tonight. She has to make the next more. I've made it very clear how I feel.

"Get your bag and I'll take you up to the guest room. You can stay in the other guest room, not the one you freshened up in, the other one. It's larger," and as they went upstairs she continued. "There is a small bath, shower, towels and things. I keep this room ready for a guest, not so much the others."

Upstairs Dan put his bag down and said, "This is a nice guest room, a big bed, big chair. I like it. Much better than the Windham."

Chris said, "I'm glad you like it. I have to go back downstairs and get the doggies ready for bed and check the fireplace. Make sure the outside lights are on. Bedtime stuff."

"I'll go with you, in my flowing robe," he said as he laughed.

"It fits pretty good. I don't know who it belonged to. My brothers are all tall too."

They went together and did all the night time duties.

They went back up the winding staircase and upon reaching the top he kissed her lightly on the cheek. He was afraid of a close embrace. He would not want it to end.

"I'm going to take a nice hot shower and retire with my book," he told her.

"That is exactly what I'm going to do."

"Sleep well, sweetie and . . . if you're ready for a third nap you know where to find your napping partner," he said slowly and again kissed her on her cheek.

She only smiled.

She knew what he was saying or asking. She had never completely made love to Brian. They wanted to wait for that special moment, after they were married. But that special moment was snapped from their lives never to be completed. This had plagued Christina since he so quickly left her life and left it unfulfilled.

After his shower Dan got into the big bed that was his for the night. He decided not to read. He lay in the dark looking at the ceiling and just thinking.

Christina too went to her bedroom and prepared for sleep. The storm had finally passed and it was only raining lightly. She opened her window a bit. She could hear the large oaks moving gently against the house. Most of the night sounds were in another part of the world. Fall always holds a strange peacefulness, a tranquility that lies dormant unless disturbed by something. She was aware that the peacefulness in her body had become restless. She could feel it wanting to respond to love and to Dan.

She got up and in the dark walked slowly to the guest room. She tapped lightly on the door.

"Are you asleep?" she asked softly.

"No, come in," he replied. Oh god how I love her and now I can tell her with my touch and with my body and not just words, he thought. She slowly closed the door and made her way to the bed and to Dan. She slipped in beside him where he truly had no pajamas and softly said, "Make love me."

His arms welcomed her and they lay oh so close for moments and moments. They whispered softly to each other and he easily took the sheer nighty from her warm and soft body and love was theirs alone.

♥

Morning arrived and the rain had stopped but the house was shrouded in fog. A night of love had kept them sleeping late.

Dan awake took her in his arms and said playfully, "Now you have to marry me."

She giggled and nodded her head still in the pillow. "I had better go take care of the dogs." She got out of bed and reached for the robe that she had given Dan last night.

"I'll be back or do you want to get up," she asked.

"Please come back, just for a little while," he warmly answered.

Henry and Daisy cared for she went back. A little while turned into an hour or so. In the quietness of the house and closeness of the fog, they once again belonged to each other.

"Morning is almost gone," Chris said. "I'll get dressed and make coffee and breakfast."

She left Dan alone to get dressed. By himself a thousand and one thoughts ran through his mind. All blanketed in joy, but mostly elated that she would marry him. Making plans for the future with her will be the best plans I've ever made.

He continued his happy thoughts on this gray morning, but his heart was bright with sunshine. Loving her could never be better but he knew as the years go by love always grows and theirs would also.

For Dan his love for Christina was very special. It was his first true love and his heart was so full of happiness and he wanted her to feel that way too.

With wonderful thoughts he went down to the kitchen where Christina had made coffee and breakfast. He took her in his arms and said, "I love you so very much Christina."

She said, "I love you too . . . but," and he quickly put his finger over her lips to stop the next words.

"That is all I want to hear." He kissed her long and they held each other close.

"Did I hear coffee?"

She shook her head and wrinkled her nose, "Yes, and a few other things to go with it."

"This kitchen table is as big as the dining table," he said. They sat across from each other and enjoyed breakfast together.

"What about those guys," and he pointed to the dogs.

"They had their breakfast but they hope I forgot and will feed them again. So they wait patiently for a bite. They're sweet."

"Did you make any plans for today," he asked.

"No, I thought I could meet you in town, but . . . that is not a plan anymore," said with expression as she laughed.

"Loving you last night and today made me the happiest man in the world."

"It's new for me," she added softly and shyly.

He replied ever–so–gently, "I know . . . but together we can grow and know each other in every way."

She was telling him in her own way that it was the first time anyone had completely made love to her. He knew and felt somewhat relieved that he was her first love as she was his.

They lingered at the kitchen table for quite some time talking and laughing. Finally Dan asked, "Would now be a good time for you to show me your paintings."

"If you really want to."

"I very much want to see them. Also I want to go out and take some pictures before this fog lifts. It makes a great backdrop for just about anything."

"We, meaning the dogs, can go with you."

"You can show me some spots where you've taken pictures or painted and I can capture them in the fog."

"Let's go now, the fog is still rather thick. You'll get wonderful shadows."

♥

With camera in hand and dogs at their side they walked all around the house and up the hill, down toward the barn.

Dan took many shots of the trees, in the haze, the dogs running. On the path he turned and said,

"Stand there sweetie, the shadows behind you will be a good backdrop."

And he took several more of her. "I want to take some of you inside."

The dogs seemed ready to go in, as did Dan and Chris, because it was a bit cool and wet after the rainy night.

"Are we staying home this afternoon?" he asked.

"Whatever you want to do?" she replied.

"Let's stay in, unless you want to go out to eat."

"I have plenty things to eat."

"I want to see your paintings and then relax in that beautiful library, take some more pictures of you and your dogs, have dinner, there is a lot to do. And maybe take a quick little nap," and he smiled lovingly at her.

She responded with a willing smile.

"Paintings first."

"Yes."

"They're all in my brother's room. Papa and I have also been discussing what to show at the gallery We have chosen different ones, but that is individual preference. Now we'll have your opinion," she said as they went upstairs.

At the end of the long hall they entered the "display" room as Christina had called it. There were some twenty paintings sitting on the floor, on tables and on chairs.

As his eyes scanned the room, he exclaimed, "Oh! This is quite a collection. They're beautiful. I can see why you're having a hard time choosing. Oh my," Dan was truly overwhelmed.

He noticed most of them were landscapes but a few were stills.

He started at one end and was about to carefully look closely at each one when Chris gave him a chair. She sat down in another by the door.

He carefully looked at each one. Pointing out things that he especially liked and asking her when she did them. He soon realized that they were arranged in chronological order. He also realized the first ones were bright and full of color. Nature's spring, summer greens, flowers, bright fall colors as they presented themselves. Even the winter snow was bright. And then, as he moved around the room he noticed that all things colorful had turned dull, lifeless. Although they were dynamic there was a death about them. This wasn't just one painting but a group. He glanced at the entire group again and found the more recent ones were bright again.

He thought, why?

"Chris, the paintings you did about two years ago seemed dark and lifeless. Was that just a look you were trying to capture, were you experimenting?" he asked.

"Oh, I don't know, I hadn't noticed. Papa mentioned that too. Just the way I felt, I guess," she responded vaguely. But she knew very well why her paintings were so dark, but she did not feel like sharing with Dan now or never.

In his mind Dan questioned her response. This dark period was so evident, she should have a better answer. If she was experimenting with capturing darkness, she would easily explain. Although her mother had passed a few years earlier, he thought she would have been forthright in talking about that.

Of course Dan noticed this because of his attention to details. He wondered if something dark had happened in her life. Her response had been so casual he wasn't ready to accept it.

About an hour passed and after Dan had carefully perused each one he said smiling, "I think I have chosen my ten. Although there is something striking and wonderful about each one."

With that he pointed out his favorites. He told her why he had chosen these and why not the others. She found his observations very interesting. She was about to take a new look at several. He had even selected one from the dark period. The one he chose from that time was a sunset that seemed to be on fire and screaming for help. Dan being a photographer thought it a sunset. Then he knew for sure, she called it, "After Sunset."

This was the first of her paintings from the dark time in her life. This was the first painting she did after losing Brian. It had been a leap into grief and it continued for quite some time.

The day she finished the painting she wrote in her diary that had been devoted only to him.

Dear Brian
Today I finished After Sunset not from seeing but from remembering. It was the first sunset I saw after your passing. It's like my heart, on fire as I said goodbye to you . . . Once the sun was golden like you and brought a glow of happiness . . . you were my

sunshine that brought a light into my being, into my young life The shards of blue are openings to your eternity through which I can send my endless love. My devotion will be everlasting till we can become soul mates and our spirits will be one for an eternity – eternity will be too short and forever not long enough to spend with you – until – I caress your golden locks that you gave so long ago – you are close I feel your presence They are you. And now you are gone as that sunset too slides into eternity never to shine again. But you shine in my heart ALWAYS and ALWAYS

My eternal love Chris

This tear stain page had been her last entry. She had started Dear Diary when she first met Brian that day at the stables. And through the years she wrote her feelings and day to day events about their time together. One day she had planned to read it to him. Without Brian there could be no Dear Diary. She had closed it some two years ago and never opened it again.

Christina then told Dan which paintings that she more or less had selected. There was much agreement.

"We have been here a long time," he said to her as he turned to her and took her face in his hands, "They're absolutely beautiful, all of them. They're poetry in color. I request one on my Christmas list."

"Thank you. I'm glad you like them. It had been one of my interests for a long time. Not knowing what else my brother John, years ago when he was in high school and me about seven, had Santa bring me a paint set. I absolutely loved it. Before that I had not shown any desire or talent to be an artist. I say that modestly."

Dan quickly responded, "John launched your career as an artist and you have much talent. I can understand why they want to hang your work in their gallery."

"I'll give you a tour of the house and there are some more around. Most of them I did when I first went to college. Mother placed them around and now papa won't let me move them. They hung them together. Their little girl's paintings. You know how moms and dads are."

"Yes, you must have noticed lots of pictures at moms," he added.

"I did, especially the tree collection in her dining room. I can't wait to see more. They're beautiful."

As they walked through the house she pointed out her paintings.

"There is one in my bedroom, if you'll excuse, the bed isn't made."

"You didn't sleep here last night. It looks fine. A good place for an afternoon nap," he said as he glanced at her with a coy expression. She said nothing but raised her eyes into her brow.

"I realize you're not quite hungry yet but I have a frozen chicken casserole that I made a couple days ago. How does that sound and I'll make a salad to go with it," she asked Dan.

"Perfect."

In the library Dan asked, "Would you like for me to make a fire?"

"Sure, and what would you like to hear. We'll brighten this day with music," but rather what she chose was totally romantic and it set the mood.

Dan had the fire going and Chris the music, he reached for her and said, "May I have this dance?"

She easily slipped into his arms and they went through the motions.

He whispered to her. "You're hair smells so good. I can say that now that I know you better."

She looked at him with those eyes that never stop.

"Will you come to the city before I go to London? I have no commitments on the weekend before I go."

They stopped their dance and Dan reached in his wallet and got out his tiny calendar. He read the days that he would be free from work, and could come out if she had no plans.

Christina thought he is really taking up all my spare time. But oh, how I love being with him. She still questioned his sincerity, not by the way he acted or what he said, but their relationship was moving rather fast. And do things like this really last? Do they slowly end before they can get a firm hold in the heart? She compared this short amount of time with Dan to the ten years that she had been with Brian. It only took Dan several days to realize what had been so much longer with Brian. Do you really fall in love so fast? Is it a love for all the days we will have together?

"The next two Saturdays, that's okay. Papa will be home on Sunday. So we will have only Daisy and Henry to lend our attention to on Saturday."

"That sounds good. I have already informed Kate, my agent, no weekend work after I come back from London."

"Did you tell her why?"

"No, but she looked at me and gave me that knowing smile. And probably thought, at last."

A little while longer they made an attempt to dance. More than to dance it was a reason to hold each other close.

"When can I take some pictures of you? I need them to take to London with me. Personal use only," and he laughed. "The day is moving on."

"I'll put the casserole in the oven and it will be ready when we are."

"Where do you want to take the pictures?"

"I liked that bench you have in your bedroom and can we put it under the family pictures in the hall."

"I suppose so."

They got the bench and placed it under the pictures. He posed her and asked, "May I slip your blouse off your shoulders?"

As he did Christina closed her eyes as she felt his warm hand on her body. She loved the moment.

After he positioned her as he wanted her, he took several shots, her smiling, looking up, looking away.

"These will be good."

While she was still sitting on the bench he kneeled down in front of her and parted her legs and she put her arms around his waist and drew him close. He kissed her neck and then gently kissed her breast.

He looked at her with sparkling eyes and softly said, "Want to take that little nap. Last night I could only feel you as I made love, but today I can see your beautiful body."

Christina thought she would explode. Never have I felt like this and he's so beautiful. He seems to know exactly what to say and when and how to do it.

They got up, hand–in–hand they walked to Christina's bedroom. Dan adjusted the blinds but left a gentle light. She quietly closed the door.

She walked into his arms and he said, "This is our little world where we can love each other and touch each other, caress . . . until we know we are ready to come together and be one."

Christina felt completely relaxed and she wanted Dan to know this. She wanted to make him feel as passionate as he had made her feel.

"May I give you a back rub?" she asked.

"Please do."

They undressed each other in the twilight of the late afternoon. They stood before each other and he held her small breast in his hands and kissed her waiting lips. Not wanting him to stop but she said "Turn around I promised you a back rub." She massaged his back and then ran her hands down his side and then to the front of his body. There she caressed his stomach and then her hands touch where he most desired. She fondled him ever go gently. He felt his whole body come alive in one small moment.

"I don't want this to be over too soon." He turned and lifted her into her bed. "I want this to be about us, not just me," he whispered.

They touched and caressed each other's body. He kissed her everywhere and she returned the favor. With their passion at its highest they completed their love for each other.

They had truly loved each other passionately. They had exhausted each other, although they felt wonderful and sad it was over. They lay very still and so close they could feel every curve, every pulse, every rise and fall of each other's body. Time was theirs and they did not want it to end.

But finally Dan said, "How about a soothing shower before we eat. And I don't want to but I have to think about getting back to the city. But now a shower."

Christina's shower was not too large but they smiled and laughed and washed each other— everywhere.

Dressed, they made their way to the kitchen and to tend to the dogs and to eat.

"I have to work early on both those Sundays, that we talked about earlier, but I can come out for the Saturday." He informed her.

"That's all right."

"This magazine I am working for is very particular. They tell us our work is okay then they call at the last minute and say they want something done over. This is when we have to do some weekend work. It will be done soon and I'll be so glad."

"Is the kitchen table okay for dinner?" she asked.

"My dear, you know any table, anywhere. It's to be with you that's important."

They ate heartily after such a busy day. "These two days have been unbelievably wonderful. We were able to be alone, get to know each other more . . . and better. Going forward will be the best time of our lives. I'm so glad you came to my bedroom. I wanted you to want me as much as I wanted you."

"After all it was easy and I just couldn't leave you all alone in a strange place," she said playfully.

He smiled too, "It's getting a little dark now. I had better get packed up. I don't want to leave you alone."

A bit choked up she said, "I'll be fine. I stay here by myself. Papa and I agreed that we would not be depended on each other. But then you know how Papa is." She paused. "It's okay."

"If I go by seven, I'll be home by nine and that will give me time to prepare for tomorrow."

Seven o'clock came all too soon for both of them and Dan decided that he must be on his way. He gathered his things from the guest room.

Chris got her jacket and went with him to the back garage where his car was parked.

"Let me hold you one more time—Christina love—I feel a contentment that I've never known. I thought I fell in love with you that summer evening. But the real love came these few days that we have been together. Words are beautiful but with words there must be a touch—a caress—a coming together—and when there is love the emotions becomes spiritual—our love has made us one—we belong to each other—and that is what I found these days with you. We are truly soul mates—you have completed me with your love."

"Oh love yes—yes," she so softly said as she looked into his dark and sparkling eyes and easily touched his face.

And he kissed her ever–so–gently and he was on his way.

She went into the house and with Daisy and Henry at her side, she watched Dan's car fade away in the long drive. She lingered there thinking and the music flowing around her, she broke into tears.

"Oh my I can't let this happen," she said aloud.

She went into the library and fell in the pillows on the couch and tried to stop crying. She tried so hard but nothing helped, and she cried. I should go do something and all my thoughts will go away. And it was those thoughts that had unsettled her so. All weekend I enjoyed Dan so very much, talking, walking. I enjoyed making love to him. But she felt Brian's presence just too much! Did he know what was happening Why do I feel guilty?

She reached out and Daisy had come to be by her side. She would cry and then fall nearly asleep, then wake suddenly, not knowing why. Is Brian's spirit hovering and haunting me, she thought? Is he watching me? It was all these unsettled feelings that were coming forth and she could not control them or stop crying.

She went to her bedroom, the bed still askew from her and Dan's afternoon of loving each other. She opened her dresser drawer and in the little box,

167

she reached for the curls and held them softly to her lips.

She whispered, "I'm sorry Brian, I've betrayed you."

All evening and almost all of the night she was distressed and her heart full of anguish.

CHAPTER TEN

♥

Monday morning arrived and she looked in the mirror and her eyes were almost swollen shut. I can't go to school like this she thought. Tomorrow will be better. Tomorrow always makes things better or if not better, different.

She called and said she was sick and hoped to feel better tomorrow. With that, she worked very hard at getting herself together. If I can do that I can think things out and reach conclusions agreeing or disagreeing with myself, she thought. Today will be better for everything. She spent most of the day doing little things, but the big thoughts often got in the way of reality.

In the late afternoon she felt much better when she heard the dogs bark outside. It usually was an announcement and she went to see. A small white delivery van, a florist truck, was coming up the driveway. At the door a man handed her eleven deep red rosebuds. She thanked him and she knew they had to be from Dan. His thoughtfulness had overwhelmed her from the first day they met. And they were and the card read

> To my Christina
> *"my love is like a red red*
> *rose newly sprung in June"*
> *Yours forever Daniel*

What had been accomplished this day immediately fell apart. She started to cry again.

A few minutes later the phone rang. She did not want to answer, because she was afraid it was Dan. But she did. It wasn't Dan but her friend Jan.

"Chris are you all right, you're sick?" she asked because she knew that Dan had been there for the weekend.

"I'm okay," she said in a raspy voice unlike her own.

"You sound awful," Jan responded.

With that Chris started to cry. "Oh Jan, I'm so confused."

"Is Dan still there?"

"No."

"Can I come out? You sound distressed." Jan asked.

"Yes, I need to talk. I so need to talk."

It took Jan forty–five minutes to get to Christina's house. They greeted each other with a big hug. "Oh Chris, look at you, what is the matter? Did you break up with Dan?" Jan was firing questions.

"Come on in," Chris said. "You probably haven't eaten."

Jan shook her head. "It's not important."

"I haven't either. I have some vegetable soup, rolls and apple sauce in the kitchen."

Chris got everything together and put it on the dining table and poured her heart out to Jan. Of course neither ate much.

"He came out early Saturday and we had two wonderful days together. We went to the museum, we heard an organ recital—we walked—we took pictures—I fixed a candlelight dinner—he stayed all night—we made love—and we made love. He's so wonderful," and she paused to sob.

"This all sounds absolutely wonderful, then why are you so distressed," Jan asked pathetically.

Chris answered softly, "Brian—I feel like I have betrayed him for someone I hardly know. We were together ten years and nothing happened like this weekend. I loved him so very much and yet I never had the feelings that I had this weekend with Dan. It can't be real. I feel like Brian knows what I've done. I never made love to him, we touched each other but that was all. There were times when we came close but it never really or completely happened. He wanted to protect me. I was still in graduate school."

"Since it wasn't to be, maybe it's better that you didn't make love to him. Chris, that is a part of him that you don't have to forget, a part you never knew. Making love is a very lasting feeling.

Sometimes it takes a while to go away. Oh Chris, I know you loved each other, but he is gone. He's gone! He's gone! You were very young when you met Brian but now you're older. We understand more. Does Dan know how you feel?" Jan concluded.

I don't think so."

"I'm twenty–five but I never had any other boyfriends. I never wanted any. Brian was my life from the second moment I saw him." She tried to smile.

"Chris you can't let the past so affect your future. Dan seems so nice and those roses!" Jan pointed to them.

"Yes they just came. Read the card."

"Oh Chris! I do believe he loves you. Somehow you have to break with the past. Chris you can't let this guy get away. He sounds so wonderful."

"I think he is, only if it's all true," Chris said as her breath caught.

"I feel your reluctance, but from what you have said he sounds very sincere and that he truly loves you. He is a mature man and can recognize love when he finds it. This is a starting point with you and Dan. It has started with two adults knowing what life has to offer, loving each other. When you met Brian you only fourteen and didn't understand what true love was. You met as friends and you had time to go through all of the stages to fall in love, you had to grow up. With Dan those stages are behind you. You met him as an adult and have every right to fall in love sooner."

"I don't want him to know. I'll try to do it by myself," she responded.

"I'll help you all I can," was Jan's answer. "Are you going to call him and thank him?"

"Yes I have to," Chris said. "Let's begin to get you together, I know you want to," Jan decided.

"I was doing okay until the roses arrived. And I feel better that you're here. I have to go to school tomorrow. Who was there for me?"

"Mrs. Dietrich."

"Did anyone know that Dan was here for the weekend?" Chris asked Jan.

"No, I don't believe so. I don't think anyone knows that you are even seeing him. No buzz," Jan acknowledged. "But everyone knows that we're close and probably wouldn't say much to me. Carrie mentioned that your papa was gone and hoped everything was okay. But that is all I heard."

"That's good. I'm not about to tell the world about this yet and maybe never. Things have to be resolved. I have to resolve them."

"We'll start this moment and get you together."

And it was only then they finished their dinner.

"Want some trifle. I made it for Saturday. There is some left."

"Oh yes, I like trifle. I believe you brought some to school once and I really liked it." Chris got a small dish for both of them.

Chris realizing talk had all been about her she asked, "Have you seen Richard?"

"No, but we talked on the phone. I'm not sure I want to resume our courtship," Jan said firmly. "Being away from him this summer gave me time to think and I don't want to start seeing him again. He is just to abrasive. That is for later. I want you to get this straightened out in your mind and go forward with Dan. Do you really like him, if not this story is over?"

"Oh yes!" Chris quickly answered. "I love him, but then again I'm afraid to. It is happening so fast. And then too much of Brian is still with me and just won't go away," she firmly said.

"Look," Jan said, "Maybe he hasn't gone away because there hasn't been a reason for him to go away. And now there is a reason—Dan. A very good reason. Free your heart for him."

"Today is today and we'll see what the next and the next brings," Chris said and she wondered if it made sense. "He's coming out next Saturday just for the day. He has to work Sunday. Papa will be home Sunday. Also he wants me to come to the city for the weekend before he goes to London. He'll be gone for about a month. Maybe that will give me the time that I need to get things straightened out in my mind."

"Oh Chris, keep seeing him and loving him and you'll want what's here and what you can touch and hold close. It will be wonderful for you," Jan said lovingly with pain in her voice. "Chris I envy you in a good sort of way. Gosh it's getting late. Are you going to call Dan?" Jan asked. "I want to be here after you quit talking because I don't want you to cry again. Call him now. Go in the library and I'll wait here."

"Do I sound like I've been crying?"

"No, you sound better. If he asks anything tell him the rain from yesterday made you hoarse," Jan reasoned and she smiled.

"Good excuse, he'll want to rush out here and take care of me."

Jan waited while Christina went into the library to call Dan.

"Dan its Chris," she started. "I got the rosebuds and they're magnificent, they're beautiful, and I thank you with all my heart again and again."

"Oh my darling Christina, they're so small compared to how I love you. I'm glad you like them. Anyway how was your day?"

"Good, nothing exciting, ordinary day." She managed to say convincingly. "How about yours?"

"Okay, but I had a hard time keeping my mind on what I was doing. Your beautiful face and the beautiful things we did, kept a smile on my face all day."

She couldn't tell him that she too was lost in what they did and said. This and others had encompassed her since he left, along with a lot of tears.

"I can hardly wait for next Saturday. How about if I call you Thursday. I never know what time I'll be home. But if all goes well I can be there early Saturday. You can plan the day but save time for a long nap. You will?"

"I will. I will," she said as she laughed and it was probably the first time since he left.

"I'll call Thursday and good night and sleep as if I was at your side."

"Good night my dear and I love you," she meant what she said but she had to force those words.

Dan was content that he could make her happy. This is what he wanted to do from this day and until forever. But he felt there was something missing. Whatever it is, if anything, we'll overcome it. He hoped as time goes by this feeling would fade into somewhere forgotten. He thought maybe time is a factor for her. It hasn't been very long since we first met.

Christina hung up the phone and she told herself, there is absolutely nothing to cry about except happiness and she went to the dining room where Jan was waiting.

She sat down at the table and Jan asked, "How did it go?"

"It went all right, I don't believe I sounded funny."

"Are you sure you're all right?"

"Yes, I think I have everything under control, at least for now," Christina assured her.

"I should have brought clothes and I could stay with you tonight. I don't want you to start crying again."

"No, I really feel so much better. It was something I had to get out and I think it is, at least it is working its way to an end."

Christina assured Jan that she was all right. So she got ready to go.

"I'll see you first thing tomorrow."

They hugged and Jan was gone.

Chris was exhausted from the busy weekend and also from her feeling so despondent, but found sleep waiting.

♥

Christina went to school the next day and her composure was without flaw. She felt she had to be that way for she did not want anyone, other than Jan, to know her emotional dilemma.

Jan stopped by early to make sure she was there and doing okay. She found her in good spirits and said she would stop by after classes, when all the students were gone.

Jan, true to her word, and after the long day and the halls were empty she went to Christina's room.

"Did it go okay?" Jan asked.

"It was a struggle at times, but yes."

"Do you want me to go home with you tonight?" Jan asked.

"Would you! Two nights, if you don't have other plans," Christina pathetically responded. "I feel okay but you are so good to talk to."

"I can stay two nights, if you want me to," Jan said.

That would be good. Then I have photography club Thursday. I volunteered again this year."

"Why don't you follow me to my house and I'll get some clothes and we can go on to your house. Want me to bring food."

"No I have plenty," Chris assured her.

And the girls were off to get Jan's clothes and on to Christina's for the night.

As they sat at the dining table doing their lesson plans and enjoyed the rosebuds, Christina glanced at a picture of her maternal grandmother. My mother looked so much like her. Reminders like this make it so hard to let go. I don't mean forget, we never do, but let things rest. Papa seems to have."

"When you love so deeply it is even harder. Your mother and father had many years together. And there has to be a peace to that. You were cheated of time with her, but . . ."

"Mother left so quickly. She wasn't even sick. I had no preparation. No goodbye. I was just in college and I found this little white, leather-bound book and each page started with *I Love You Today Because,* and I had all of the pages filled in and was going to give it to her for her birthday. But it was too late. I put it in her casket for her to read on her journey. My goodbye to her, I cupped my hands on her face, as I had done so many times before and whispered, Mother, I love you so very much."

"Oh Chris, that is so beautiful, " Jan said as she wiped a tear from her eye and though she is breaking my heart, but she needs to talk. I'll listen till the sun comes up if it will help her heal.

"Brian helped me and he was so tender and caring. He knew what it meant to lose a loved one. Then he left so suddenly, too. There has never been anyone to help me get over him"

"My first loss was awful for me, too. I was eleven, living in a perfect world. It was a jolt into reality. My dog Betsy. Papa took her to the vet several times but one day did not bring her home. They called me into the library and explained that she was very sick and if she lived she would be in a lot of pain. And we have to think of her before ourselves. I started to cry and asked why didn't they let me say goodbye. I don't remember exactly what they said.

178

After a while I went and lay on my bed and just stared at the ceiling. All I could think of was, my best friend was gone. Then John came in and I knew my best friend was right here with me. He stayed with me for a long time without saying a word. Later that day he took me for ice cream and we talked about how much fun we had had with her. The next night I dreamed that she was scratching at my window and I was so happy, but when I opened it she was not there."

"Oh Chris, remembering can be so good sometimes even though it is bittersweet. When did Chloe and Sable come to live with you?"

"That was so sweet. About two months later, one Saturday morning Papa ask me if I wanted to go with him. I said yes, without even knowing where. We drove for a while, we talked, but I began to wonder where we were going. As he turned in a drive I saw a large wooden cut–out of a German shepherd. I knew. And when Papa said that I could pick out a brother and sister, my world began again."

"Chris, love is love. You are about to have another beginning. Let it happen. Don't be afraid."

The week went by rather fast for Christina. The photography club starting, school in general and Jan were all contributing factors in helping her get back to feeling like herself.

After Christina got home Thursday Dan called and said they planned to be through working around six tomorrow.

"I can leave from there, if that is all right. It won't be early but I'll treat you to a late dinner."

179

"That's fine but if it's late, do you really want to go out. I can fix something. Let me do that," she responded warmly.

"All right whatever you want to do. Then I'll see you tomorrow evening. I love you Chris."

"Daniel you're my love too."

Friday in school she confided to Jan that Dan was coming out tonight instead of tomorrow. Jan could tell that she was quietly elated and she could tell that Chris had felt better as the week went along.

After school Christina shopped for food. She thought Dan should sleep with me tonight, so I won't have another bedroom to get in shape before papa comes home. I'll tell him that Dan stayed all night, or should I.

All things in order and dinner waiting she watched for car lights from the big window. It was not long until they appeared. He stopped in front of the house and she and the dogs went out to meet him.

Before he said a word, he took her in his arms and held her close. "Can I say it again, I could hardly wait to get here."

"I've missed you this week and so glad you didn't have to work late today." They kissed each other fondly.

"I opened the back garage door. Why don't you drive around now and you won't have to come out again," she suggested.

"Come on, get in the car and ride with me," he said happily.

They got in the car and he drove to the back garage with doggies trailing.

"You are probably hungry and tired. Working all day and then driving out here."

"I am," and she could hear the tired in his voice.

"Can I assume you fixed dinner, that is why we're putting the car in the garage," he asked hoping she would say yes.

"Beef stroganoff, vegetables and a salad, a different kind."

Dan grabbed his bag and they went into the kitchen. Bag on the floor, he held her once more and kissed her long. Her surrender in his arms was a loving welcome and pure happiness for Dan.

"How about a glass of wine in the library to get the day behind us," she suggested.

"That's just what I brought," he said as he reached into his bag and pulled out a bottle of wine.

Music playing, they snuggled on the couch for a while and got caught up on the past week, although Christina told him only of the good things that had happened and he especially liked hearing about the photography club.

"Maybe sometime I can come out and give a little talk."

"James, the young man at your reception, saw your interview and asks if I did and did I remember you. It was too funny. I could hardly contain myself and I had to be careful not give myself away.

Mr. Clark, who is charge, also saw the interview and had your books and he discussed the composition of the photos. He did a great job of explaining how you used different elements to frame, highlights, things like that. It really held their interest. I was so proud of you and couldn't say a thing."

"Thank you. How about a little dinner?"

The rosebuds were still on the dining table and they dined in their shadow. They were beginning to open.

The dogs were on their best behavior and when Dan and Christina had finished eating he helped her get the kitchen in order. By then it was late.

"Where do you want me to put my robe and stuff, the guest room?" and they both laughed.

"You are not a guest, you're my love. Put them in my room. Sleep with me tonight," she said as she looked into his sparkling dark eyes.

"I accept. How about now, it's late and we both have had a busy week."

"Yeah, I'm so glad you could come out tonight."

Together they got everything ready for the night, outside lights, dogs and night light under the big window.

They went upstairs to Christina's bedroom. They undressed each other and he massaged her sensual body as she stood close. She touched and caressed him with her warm hands.

"How about a shower."

She smiled and nodded with raised eyes.

In the shower the warm water sprayed lightly on their bodies. They washed each other, dried and gently got into bed.

They relaxed for a while just holding each other and talking softly. Their warm lips met again and again. He gently caressed her breast and then her stomach and where she would have the feeling like nothings else he could give her. She fondled him where he could not hold back. And "I love you . . . I love you so much," were his last words as he gently moved to be one with her and again they knew their love for each other.

♥

Morning broke with the bright sun slanting through the blinds. She was cradled with her back in his arched body. They had slept that way all night. This cool September morning they snuggled together. Still cradled he ran his hand up and down the front of her body.

Dan remembered. "This is so much different than the last time we woke together, the fog."

She turned over and faced him. "I think it is also going to be warmer today."

They lay quietly just smiling at each other. She touched his face and ran her fingers around his ear. She put her hand under his arm and down his side. Dan rolled her on her back and parted her legs and touched her over and over to excite her. And that he did. She touched and fondled him with care where he wanted. And with excitement and desire their bodies again met as one.

At last they decided to shower, dress and have breakfast and start their day together.

They both had a very busy week so they decided to stay home. He helped her around the house. They took a long walk with dogs and cameras. The leaves were beginning to take on their colors of fall. They could take pictures of the same as before but it would be a new and different look. The dogs enjoyed their company. They liked having someone to throw sticks and run with them. Dan missed not having a dog, in the city and his unsettled work schedule did not allow this. Unlike Christina, she had never been without that special friend.

Another day together amid laughter and fun they prepared dinner. They ate in the kitchen at the big harvest table where they could watch the sun slowly sink into the distant trees. And to complete the day, in the quiet of her bedroom, they loved each other one more time

Before Dan left for home they talked about next Saturday. "Your papa will be home and we can go out and do something. I want you to come to the city for a weekend before I go to London. There is a lot to do and we can be alone and together and do what we like best."

"I'd like that and will look forward to it," she replied. "What day do you leave?"

"On the twelfth, but before that I work every day accept that Saturday, Sunday and the holiday. They want all the picture taking done early, so anything that has to be done over, they'll have time before that weekend," after reviewing his schedule, he asked, "How about the weekend before I go. Monday is Columbus Day and you don't have school."

"That's a good time."

"Come early Saturday morning and we can do lots and more. Is there anything special you would like to do? I'll put it on the calendar."

"No, I'll let you plan. You know all the nice things and where to go."

"I'll make you a little map to my house. It's fairly easy, on this end of the city."

"I'm anxious to see where you live."

"It's small, first floor a large living room, small kitchen, nook for eating. One bedroom. A small cellar area. When my folks come over, I sleep on the couch but it's fine for one person."

The time was passing and it had grown dark. Dan decided that he must say goodbye and be on his way home. He had an early day tomorrow. They said their goodbyes in the back where his car was parked.

Christina went in and as so many times before watched from the big window as the little red light faded into dusk.

She felt sad that Dan was leaving but happy for the time they had just spent together. She thought, this time I will think of only the good things. How close we have been. How I felt when he touched me. The things he whispered to me. His more–than–warm body. His more–than–warm body in mine. I believe things are getting better for me. She hugged herself and smiled.

CHAPTER ELEVEN

♥

Sunday, and a beautiful day. The sun was bright and leaves were beginning their autumn dress. Today papa will be home. It had been a rough time while he was gone, and she was glad he had not been here to witness her upset. She wasn't entirely over all her problems as she viewed them, but she knew she was better.

Christina and Ellen went to the airport to get Papa Zeller. His plane was due to arrive at four o'clock and it was only a few minutes late.

Christina had truly missed him but she was glad that he could visit John. Papa was getting older and probably would not be able to travel alone all too soon. She was also glad that he had been away because she and Dan were together in her home undisturbed. Had papa not planned his visit at this time, well things would not have happened the way they did. And the way they happened had been very nice, very wonderful and all very natural, she thought.

Riding home papa told the girls all about his trip. John and Rachel had taken him everywhere. He had been out there once before but loved seeing everything again. He enjoyed his granddaughters even more this time, they were a little older and they pampered him without pause and he loved the attention. Last time he had visited, he more or less had to take care of them, this time the role was reversed.

"Plans are on for them to be here for Christmas," Papa said. "I believe all the boys will be here," and directed to Chris, "Will Dan be here?"

"Well we haven't talked about Christmas yet. We have to get him back from London."

Papa asked Ellen what she had been doing and she mentioned her volunteered work, church social, and that she had completed several hats and mittens for the children of need.

"Ellen you should teach me to knit. That is one thing mother never did."

"Anytime, I have yarn, needles and all the things you need."

"After Christmas, it would be a good winter project."

It was late in the afternoon and Christina suggested, "If you are not too tired Papa, let's all go to dinner. You can finish telling both of us about your trip and everything you did."

"I'm okay. We'll not have to cook," he responded.

"How about the Cedar Grill? They have good food and it's on the way home."

Both Papa and Ellen liked the suggestion.

Papa was delighted to keep talking about John, Rachel and the girls. Christina especially wanted to hear all about what they had been doing before and while papa was there.

After dinner they took Ellen home.

As Papa Zeller and Christina drove to their home, he continued talking about John, the girls and how they pampered him. He asks Chris if everything was all right and if anything exciting had happened while he was gone.

Well, Christina thought, much has happened but I probably shouldn't tell you just now. Although she said Dan had been out a couple times.

Papa did not ask any questions of a personal nature. He kept his conversation to, did you go to the museum, what has Dan been filming?

"How did school go, did it get off to a good start?"

"Everything went well. I have a good group of students. The photo club started and I am going to help again this year. Overall it was good."

Chris kept her answers long and hoping he would not ask something she did not want to talk about. They were soon home and nothing personal had to be discussed.

At home papa was greeted exuberantly by Daisy and Henry, they had also missed him very much. Christina told papa what she had on her schedule for the week and that Dan would be coming out next Saturday to spend the day.

The week soon returned to the usual for both Christina and Papa Zeller. They each were busy with their various activities. Papa did not notice that Christina was or had been disturbed about anything.

The roses that Dan had sent Christina after the weekend that he passionately loved her were still in good condition and on the dining room table. There were only ten, Christina had taken one to her room. Papa acknowledged how beautiful they were but said nothing else. He had his own thoughts and knew what red roses meant. He hoped the best for her. Perhaps she will tell me more as time goes on, he thought.

♥

The week over and it was Saturday and Christina was awaiting Dan's arrival. They had decided to spend the day at the Shire. With Papa home it was hard to be intimate.

Dan arrived and he managed to give her a big hug and a light kiss and he whispered loving words that only she could hear. She smiled softly and replied, "All of those things and I missed you too."

They were soon on their way for a fun day at the Shire.

They looked in all of the shops and bookstores. He bought her a pair of earrings and later he put them in for her. Some of the theatres were still performing and they were fortunate to get tickets for an afternoon show. It was the musical *Showboat* It was a great performance. After the show they had dinner and arrived back at her home just at early dark.

They sat in the car for a while as Daisy and Henry circled in excitement. Dan moved over near her and their lips met. He kissed her neck as he fondled her breast. The desire between them was intense.

"We'd better go in before something happens and in the car," she said.

Dan agreed. "But let's wait just a moment."

She rolled down the window and as the fresh air rushed in, she talked to the dogs.

After a few moments they agreed that everything was back in order and they could go in.

They sat with Papa Zeller in the library for a while and he told Dan all about his trip. Then Christina suggested coffee before he had to leave. They went into the kitchen and at the table discussed her trip to the city.

"It will be two weeks before I see you again. That's an awful long time but London will be even longer. I got the pictures I took of you and the other stuff and they are wonderful. I meant to bring them but in a hurry I forgot."

He glanced at his watch and said, "It's getting late and I must go. Another early day tomorrow."

Dan said goodbye to Papa Zeller and they walked to his car accompanied by Daisy and Henry.

"It's dark and I'm sure no one is watching," he said as he took her in his arms and she too put her every being near him. "It is not my favorite way to say goodbye but for now."

This time Chris was first to say, "I love you Dan, more every day."

Cradling her in his arms, he whispered. "Until next time. I love you with everything that I can give you."

Christina stood with Daisy and Henry as Dan drove away into the night.

This time Dan was leaving very happy, but sad that he would not see her for two weeks and then a month while he would be in London. He wanted to talk to her about marriage, but decided to reserve this conversation until her visit to the big city. He thought whatever or whenever she wants, but he hoped soon. These two–hour trips were a big bite out of his time, but worth the effort. But mostly going home at night to an empty house was getting tiring. Especially, he knew he wanted to spend the rest of his life with Christina.

Although there were brief moments when she seemed to be far away and he was not sure time was helping. Yet she responded to being loved and willingly loved me back, he thought. These two emotions are contradictory and Dan did not understand why.

♥

Their two weeks had been busy for both of them, school and photographing. She knew she loved Dan but Brian's spirit would not go away. She too had been guilty keeping it close to her.

Since she and Dan had been making love he had not talked about marriage. Maybe he wasn't as sincere now as he appeared to be at first. Had he accomplished his intentions and now what? These and

191

many other thoughts were ever present as she drove to school, as she drove home and as she lay quietly in her bed at night.

By the end of the two weeks she had let herself get in a state of mild confusion. As long as Dan was near she was all right but when he was gone her thoughts became confused.

He had called often, but she could tell he was tired and they did not talk long. His conversations were casual but always ended with "I love you Christina."

While Christina was creating an emotional dilemma for herself, Dan was busy working and most of all planning a wonderful time for their long weekend in the big city. He wanted everything to be special for her first visit. Most of all he wanted her to say that she would marry him. Then, he thought, I'll buy her the biggest diamond I can find in the city, a diamond to match my love for her.

The Saturday of her arrival Dan planned a day at the zoo because she had mentioned she would like to visit it again. In the evening dinner at Crawford's and nearby there was a piano lounge where they could enjoy a wonderful jazz pianist. Sunday he wanted to take her to the Cathedral. At eleven o'clock they had a different religious service. It was an hour of music. The program might include vocal, chamber music, piano and on occasion there would be a larger ensemble. It was always different. One could find their spiritual experience or just enjoy the love of music. He had been there several times and wanted to share it with Christina when she visited. He knew how much she loved music, as much as literature.

Then brunch somewhere and two blocks over is a street of bookstores where they could easily get lost for a long time.

Monday, other than taking her out to eat, they would just be together. He would show her some of his work and the pictures that he had taken at her home and of her. He had chosen the one he liked best and it was sitting on his dresser so it would be the first thing he would see each morning. Seeing her picture would give his day a great start. A picture would have to do until he could see her every day as herself.

CHAPTER TWELVE

♥

Saturday arrived at the Zeller residence. Both Christina and Papa Zeller were getting ready to leave. Papa's sister Mary had invited him and the dogs until Monday. She and her husband Edward lived about an hour's drive south. Daisy and Henry liked to play with their lab Junior. Papa in the driver's seat and Daisy and Henry sitting stately in the back, Christina saw them off. She was also ready and decided to be on her way.

The drive to the city was pleasant. The sun was bright and the loose fluffy clouds wandered easily through the endless sky. The trees were more and more into fall. Golds, rusts and deep reds were everywhere. She thought there is beauty in all seasons, but the vibrancy of the colors so alive yet on their way to death. The music from the radio included Rachmaninoff, Chopin and others. Hearing music that she and Brian had shared made his spirit feel even more present and this feeling was always stronger when she was away from Dan.

Being with Dan for these days would bring her back to where she wanted to be. Until now regardless how much she seemed to love him, her thoughts of Brian would not go away. Perhaps if I knew he was totally sincere, that would help make things right, she thought. Something from Dan would have to be stronger than the ten years with Brian. For her, time had not healed as it should.

As she drove the skyline of the big city came into view. She would begin following the little map that Dan had sent her. It seemed to be accurate as she went along. Every turn and every corner was just where it should be.

Soon she arrived at the street where Dan lived. She had arrived earlier than they planned. The houses were all brownstone in character. The tall trees created a cozy neighborhood atmosphere. She found a place to park her car. It was not in front of his house but further down the street. She got out and went around the back to get her tote from the trunk. Just then she looked up toward Dan's house and she saw an extremely attractive girl carrying a small, what appeared to be an overnight bag, with Dan close behind. They walked slowly to the end of the walk. Christina was stunned but watched. They talked and he took her hand then he took her other hand. Then Dan kissed her lovingly and she seemed to do the same and they parted. He watched her as she got into her car and drove away. He quickly turned and went back into his house.

Christina was aghast! An uncomfortable lump rose instantly in her throat, and her heart started to pound. I have arrived early and found him with someone else, she thought. If I had arrived even earlier, the situation could have been even more tragic. She got back in her car and sat there stunned. Anger and tears vied for her emotions and the tears soon won. She had been totally devastated in those few moments.

What do I do, she asked herself. I don't want to see him! Without any clear thought she started her car and drove wildly down the narrow street. All she could think of was to get out of the city and away from Dan as fast as she could, far away from him as possible. It was a false trust she had built and as she suspected he is a man of the world she did not know. She thought, Brian would never have done this to me.

Dazed and still without clear thoughts she drove for almost an hour. By then a feeling of relief came over her. All the uncertainties, questions and things to overcome were dispelled in that one brief moment. It would not be necessary for her to make a decision about Dan. He had made it for her. Her thoughts traveled back to Brian, he would not be in another's arms. He is where she could always be close and yet far away. Life would be as usual in its uncomplicated way. It was all over with Dan and most of all she would not have to forget Brian.

As she drove the day suddenly became gray, a storm was looming on the horizon. It grew darker and darker and she felt she should stop. She soon found an out–of–the–way motel where she could spend the night and regain her composure. No one would miss her and Dan would have his sweetie.

She registered, got the key and quickly found her room. She threw herself on the bed and the tears did not wait. She just wanted to clear her mind, to rid herself of the hurt that had infringed on her feelings that she so carefully guarded. In a state of half consciousness she was thinking how clever Dan must have thought himself to be.

Outside, it had turned to a storm. Wind blowing hard, rain smacked the windowpane and the thunder crashed. Chris in her state of hurt and bewilderment fell into a light sleep.

♥

Dan had spent the morning tidying his house and doing last minute things for the week-end. Although his cleaning lady had been there a day earlier, he checked to see that all things were in order. Reservations were confirmed. He made sure he had tickets for the Saturday evening of jazz. Nothing left to do but wait.

The storm that Christina had experienced earlier had reached the city. The bright sky had turned to gray and the rain and thunder began slowly only to increase as time went on. At first Dan thought it was just a passing thunder storm, but soon realized that it might be around for a while. And Christina was late. He tried to relax and wait for her to arrive. He watched out his front window for her little red car. It was twelve o'clock, yet he was not alarmed because the storm had probably slowed her down. Another

197

hour passed and the storm was still around. His concerns were growing. Another hour passed and his anxieties increased even move At worst she should have arrived long ago. He thought maybe she had to stop because of the heavy rain. Hopefully she will call if she is detained for long. Did she have an accident? He pondered many thoughts and questions.

It was getting later in the afternoon and he began pacing the floor and every minute he would look out the window. There was no doubt she should have definitely arrived by now. His concerns were extreme. His throat was dry and horrible thoughts would not leave his mind. As he looked out the window he wanted to see a car, just any car and maybe it would be hers. His thoughts had reached the panic stage. I must do something and now, what first.

He decided to call her home and verify her time of leaving. He was also concerned that his call would alarm her papa and perhaps unnecessarily. But he called. Much to his dismay no one answered the phone.

By now the storm had passed and all that remained was a heavy drizzle. This early fall rainstorm had found its way to the lake. The temperature had cooled considerably. In the immediate area there didn't seem to be any damage only large puddles of water and a few disengaged leaves.

Dan had his radio and television on but there didn't seem to be any alarm or special reports about the storm.

He was violently upset and continued to make phone calls to see if he could locate her. She could need help. First he called the state trooper and then several hospitals that were near her route. After much waiting for return calls they all said no accidents had been reported answering her description. He was relieved about one thing only to be concerned about another.

As he waited he thought of the many things that could have happened to her. Had she been kidnapped? Was her car in a ravine and she trapped in it? Was she near death in some hospital? A wrong turn could have taken her into the country and her car could have gone off the road in the storm. Did she have to walk for help in the rain on some isolated road? He was not sure of the route she took to the city. The map he had prepared for her started at the city's edge. It could be days before he would know what happened to her. He cursed himself. Why did I insist that she drive here alone?

He had exhausted all possibilities of finding her tonight. He was also puzzled that no one seemed to be at her home. Had something happened to her papa? Someone should be there sooner or later to take care of the dogs. Confusing questions and horrifying answers were haunting his mind. It grew later and later and in all of this bewilderment Dan fell asleep on his couch, fully clothed.

♥

Through a restless and erratic sleep morning finally arrived. Dan was alert rather quickly and realized he had not slept well. He thought, how could I. After a hot shower and strong coffee he felt better

199

physically but still emotionally distraught. Where is my beloved Christina he thought as he called her home thinking someone must be there by now. He turned his pacing the floor into a short walk outside. Fresh air always helps if only temporarily.

The street was quiet. Stillness hung gently in this normally busy neighborhood. It was Sunday. The air had pleasantly cooled from the rain of yesterday. The morning sun was just appearing from behind the early clouds. A slight hint of a breeze played softly among the trees. Most of the puddles of water from the rain the night before had dried. It was a delightful morning, fresh and almost spring like, but Dan could not enjoy it. He was too concerned. Where are you Christina, he asked himself? His walk was short.

He went back to his house and again made the same phone calls that he had made the night before, the state police, the local hospitals. Still no one of her description had been entered and again he called her home. The morning was agonizing for him. He continued to think about what could have happened. A new thought, had something happened to her and her papa together. Should I drive out to her home?

Dan watched television but did not see or comprehend what he was looking at. To no avail his mind wandered frantically with horrible thoughts. All he could do was wait.

♥

A hundred or so miles away Christina too had awakened to a morning of distress. She had arrived early only to find Dan with another woman. And to think I actually believed he was sincere, she thought. It's over. She had given it a chance and had been humiliated. What if I had arrived on time and I never saw what I did, how long would he have kept this fake relationship going? I have been so naïve. I'll drive home, put my car in the garage and no one will know I'm there. Papa won't call, Jan won't, Ellen won't call because everyone knows we're all gone.

For Christina the day was still gray from the storm of yesterday. She would be home soon and there would be time to recuperate from the shock of yesterday. With papa at Aunt Mary's, the house would be quiet and she could reflect. It would be certain that she would give as much thought to Brian and perhaps more, as she would to Dan. For her, both would be out of her life.

The drive home was quiet, no music to arouse her emotions. The sky was beginning to clear and puffy white clouds were scattered throughout. It held the promise of a beautiful day.

She had only been in the house a few minutes when the phone rang. She felt sure it was Dan and refused to answer. This went on all day. All day she refused to answer.

She went through the day quietly, she did not build a fire, she did not listen to music, she only came out of her bedroom to eat. Tomorrow I will answer the phone, maybe, she thought.

The day was very long for her and the night even longer. But finally Monday morning arrived. Again the phone started ringing, but she waited a few hours, and then answered.

A frantic sigh was released at the other end of the line. "Chris! Are you all right!" he asked desperately and very chocked up.

"Yes," was her quick and curt reply.

"Where were you Saturday? I was frantic when you didn't show up. Why didn't you call?" his questions were coming very quickly.

She could tell by the tone of his voice that desperation had been unleashed.

Although she hadn't planned what she was going to say she quickly decided to come right out and tell him she had arrived early and found him saying goodbye to a woman. "It appeared she had stayed all night equipped with bag and all." She was mildly frantic. Her voice shaking and her stomach in a knot as she unleashed her anger. Dan sensed her rage and stopped her before she would say something she would be sorry about later.

"Oh no darling, that was only Eleanor. We had to do some shots over and I thought we could do them quickly Saturday morning early before you came. We've worked together many times. She did not stay all night. She is a colleague. I walked outside with her and I was telling her that you were coming up and how excited I was. Darling I love you. I'm not interested in anyone else. Why do we misunderstand each other?"

As he was talking Chris felt more and more that she had deluded herself by what she saw.

"I don't want this conversation to go on any longer on the phone. I can be there in a couple hours. I'm as good as in my car. Okay!" He paused only to determine if she was still listening.

♥

It was just two hours later when Christina looked out the big window only to see Dan's car in the long drive. A few minutes later he was on the porch and through the open door. He quickly took her in his arms and held her close. She did not respond. Five minutes or so passed before they spoke. Holding her by the shoulders and speaking directly into her eyes, "Oh Chris, I'm so sorry that you misunderstood. I was so looking forward to your visit and being with you. You're the love of my life. How can I be more clear!"

He continued with strong words. "I spent the worse two nights of my life. I imagined all sorts of bad things happening to you. I couldn't get your father. Where is he? Where are the dogs? Did you come straight home?"

"No," she replied in a quiet voice. "I stayed at the motel in Grafton. It was storming. I saw you coming out of your house with a girl and then kiss her. I thought you had deceived me." She was working hard to hold back the tears.

She backed away and glanced down. "I was hurt once and I can't be hurt again." She turned and walked into the large living room. Dan followed.

"Oh!" Dan said surprised. "I won't ever hurt you. Do you want to talk about it?" With those words he began to understand many things. Analyzing her actions and words he felt there was something in the past that caused her unresponsive moments.

"No!" she stated quickly and emphatically. "I should never have mentioned it!"

With a quick turn she took his hand and said, "I'm the one that should be apologizing."

He pulled her close and stopped her words by placing his finger upon her lips.

After a long pause she replied with a raspy and choked voice. "This has all happened so quickly I hardly know what to say. I just don't seem to know myself or what I should do. I am so confused."

"What are you confused about? Is it me? If so, I can quickly answer any questions that are confusing you," he replied.

"That is the worst part I don't even know," she said hesitating. Although Christina did know why she was confused but she did not feel like discussing it with Dan. It had become a double confusion.

In this short time of knowing him was his emotions guiding his words and actions and was his heart totally honest. She knew of his family and his career but she felt she did not know his inner self. There had not been enough time for this to develop.

The other confusion was that feelings for Brian had not gone away with time as they should have. Why . . . she did not know? Time had not healed as they say. At times love for him had grown stronger.

These were her thoughts as she stared out the big window that had witnessed so many of her private moments.

Dan was bewildered by her distant emotions. He tried to carry on a casual conversation but her answers were short and had tinges of melancholy. He was totally baffled by her turn from absolute warmth a short while ago, to a distant chill. From what she said there definitely had been someone else in her life. Her actions last Saturday were played out in what she wanted to see and not the truth. She would not talk and that left Dan completely at a loss, what to believe or what to do. He felt he simply could not reach her.

Chris fixed sandwiches and coffee as the hours grew late. She gazed out the kitchen window as she tried to eat. The food seemed to get stuck in both of their throats.

He was the only one talking but at least she was listening. "I have to go to London in two days and a separation for a month does not seem good. Leaving on such a low note, darling not good."

He continued. "I would like to resolve this great confusion but I don't know what it is to be resolved."

The remainder of the conversation was trite and to the point. Although she cleared up the mystery, where is your papa and the dogs?

Finally, Dan said that he should be getting back to the big city. As they moved to the door Dan, took her face in his hands and looked into her soft brown eyes and said, "Christina love, I love you more than you know. Whatever is bothering you, please let's talk about it. I want to help you but I have to know. If there is someone else, then I have to go. But I'm not going without a fight. I'll be gone for about a month. I will write a note . . . often. Hopefully this will give you time to resolve or decide what is coming between us."

Once more he took her in his arms and she warmly responded and they were close for moments. He kissed her lightly on her cheek. "I love you Christina. The words are the same but the meaning becomes deeper each time I say them to you."

She watched him walk swiftly to his car. He turned briefly and seeing her at the big window, he waved. She answered with a slight wave also, but he did not see her respond.

So strongly she felt this too was another last goodbye.

She went to the library and fell on the couch and hid her face in a pillow. I want to love him alone but this large shadow hangs over me. Her heart cried loudly. Make it go away! MAKE IT GO AWAY!

When she finally opened her eyes, dark had arrived. She thought papa and the dogs will be home any time and I can't be upset.

She went to the big window and there were car lights coming up the long drive. It had to be Papa, Daisy and Henry.

Papa drove to the garage in the back and she went to meet them. They had a big hug for each other. Daisy and Henry seemed happy to be home. They couldn't stop running through the house.

Papa soon sensed that she was upset. Boldly he asked, "What went wrong?"

At first she hesitated, but she then told her papa everything.

Her father knew of her profound grief of losing Brian and he also felt she had never let it find its proper place in her heart. There had never been a reason to give him up, so she never did.

He talked to her a long time telling her about losing his love, her mother. "Nothing ever replaces them in your life and in your heart, but a division takes place and they have gone one way and we are forced to go another. There is no other choice. It's what life dealt us. Fate left your life empty and you have every right to fill that void . . . And you know I cried for days and days . . . I didn't want to believe she was not here. All these feelings are natural when you love someone, but there must come a time when you have to realize this love is no longer alive, only spiritual . . . you must give it to its proper place . . . you must not let it interfere with a life that you can touch and hold. Dan seems like a wonderful person. I hope you haven't lost him. Your friendship has only begun."

She felt far away but she heard what her papa was saying.

He continued, "What life deals us is fate. We can't let it consume us, we must meet it head on and deal with it. You don't have to forget Brian, nor will you, but there is a corner of your heart waiting for him and you have to help him find its way there—I know he was the first person you ever dated and he was the first person you ever loved and for so very long. Please Chris don't let him be the last. I know it takes a long time for these emotions to go away, but you have let them last longer than you should have. Whatever way you can, let—him—go!" With that he ended his loving words.

CHAPTER THIRTEEN

♥

Fall in the North Country had become colorless and silent. The autumn leaves were crisp and brown only to drift without effort to the dark dank earth. The woods were bare and revealing. Soft summer breezes had turned to a sharp and cutting wind. The morning cardinal and the evening thrush had ceased to sing. Dark clouds gathered often to hide the quiet blue sky. The sweet aroma of summer had slipped away leaving the air bland and indifferent. The sun set earlier and rose later. It was the end of an exciting summer A summer that was once full of bright and harmonious scattered colors had now turned gray and rigid. It was a time when nature begins its sleep or death to halt it completely.

The next day Dan sent eleven fully opened roses to Chris and the card read:

"Ah, love!
> *Would not we shatter it to bits,*
> *And then, Re-mold it*
> *Closer to the Heart's Desire!"*
> *I love you only! Daniel*

With a heavy heart, Dan left for London. He had planned a weekend of fun and being close and he wanted to talk about getting married. But instead it had been three days of disaster. She had not arrived and he did not know where she was and his driving to her home only to find her in complete distress. And the worst of all he did not know why. Had she not believed him when he told her that the lady was Eleanor and they were doing retakes for the magazine? Working for this magazine had caused him many headaches and now it might cause him to lose the love of his life. And to add to this, he would be gone for a month. He had not wanted to leave this way, but it was a commitment.

♥

Chris too felt that Dan was far away. Was that good for her or not so much? She didn't feel it was off to a good start. The distress had begun before her visit to the big city. Seeing him with another girl, she didn't know what to believe, not for her nor for Dan. For now I will put it all behind and concentrate on school, was her uncomplicated decision.

Almost two weeks had passed before Christina received any communication from Dan. Then it was just a post card telling her that he had arrived safely and had begun work.

But he signed it affectionately.

The third week had gone by and just another plain post card saying he was very busy and this time he signed only his name.

There seemed to be more than an ocean between them Dan's absence and lack of communication with him had allowed Christina to hold fast to her uncertainties. She questioned herself. Maybe I don't have any true love for Dan and it was just the sex that has enthralled me. The words on the post cards had been so empty, perhaps he too was having second thoughts about their relationship. She was not looking forward, but backward.

Slowly she was letting Brian's spirit dominate her life again, although it seemed to be different. They weren't loving memories of riding or ice cream they had shared together, but they were haunting, clouded and confusing. She would look out the big window and imagine Brian riding his bicycle up the long drive. In her mind she had silent conversations with him. In her wildest dream she would make love to him, but yet so painfully unfulfilled. She would close her eyes to rest and she would imagine him calling her. She imagined him questioning her about her new friend. She often felt he was pulling her to him and too often she seemed willing to go.

If Dan was out of my life the memories of Brian would return to the memories of old, the memories made from reality, she told herself. Anger mixed with love vied for a place in her heart. These were new emotions and feelings and they disturbed her. I'll talk this over with Jan, she said to herself, she always makes me feel better.

♥

After classes either Jan or Chris would stop by the others room before going home. Their conversation was usually light or want to do something this evening. But one day Chris turned this to a serious discussion. Chris told Jan of her haunting memories and questioned why Brian was doing this to her.

"Oh Chris, Brian isn't doing anything to you, you are doing it to yourself," Jan explained.

"I do know this, but it seems to be coming from his spirit."

"It seems like you have never really said goodbye. It's overdue! Start now! This moment, you have a new love. The best reason in the world. If you need to go to his grave and one last time, say goodbye in whatever way. But say it! I believe you have been working toward that end for a long time and now it's the time for a final farewell," and Jan concluded with, "Promise."

"I will, I will," Chris promised.

"You!" and Jan emphasized you, "Have to break this hold. Brian broke his long ago."

Chris felt better after talking with Jan as she always did. What Jan said to her was not a surprise, she knew. But hearing it from her and papa helped reinforce what she must do. They talked about this several more times and Chris said she would remember the promise to Jan and to herself.

♥

Although three weeks had passed and Christina had not been able to resolve her emotional dilemma that so shadowed her. Finally Dan's absence and her uncertainty about his feelings helped her make a decision. She felt she would never be free of Brian and with that, there could never be room in her heart for Dan or anyone else. Ever! That she would have to live without him in a life riddled with despair and emptiness. It seemed to be her fate and it appeared that she was about to accept it. Rationalizing she told herself, I tried. She decided to tell Dan she needed more time to solve the emotional problem in her heart.

When Dan goes away things will be normal again. When my feelings are not challenged there is no hurt. She seemed to close the door to the future and keep the door to the past open.

When Dan returns from London and calls, if he does, she planned to tell him—something. At this time she was not sure what, but until she could break from the past and uncertainty about him was at rest, she didn't want to see him. Maybe I'll just not talk to him at all, she thought.

Dan's presence certainly created a challenge that she did not or could not accept.

♥

Dan had arrived in London in a cloud of uncertainly. He was bewildered about what she had said and what she had not said. He couldn't think straight. Perhaps this separation was a good thing after all. Well it's happening and we'll just have to see the outcome, he thought.

At the hotel he called the agency and was given plans for the next twenty–eight days. He then wrote a postcard to Christina that he had arrived safe and would write more later.

After several days and long hours of work he arrived back at the hotel and found a message from Caroline. He was surprised but delighted to hear from her. He and Caroline had had a relationship for about two years. They had visited each other several times in the U.S. and in London. An ocean and time allowed them to drift apart. They hadn't been in contact with each other for over six months. But Dan rang her up.

"My dear, how are you and how did you know I was in town?"

"I have a friend at the agency and she told me you were coming over to work with Andrews. I just had to call."

"Well how about dinner tomorrow evening. I don't know what time I will be through working, but I can call. Would that be okay?"

She agreed, "Until tomorrow."

The next evening they met at The Crown and there was a lot to catch up on. Caroline talked about her work at the publishing house, the books that she had worked on. Her vacation to the Holy Land and what Dan was reluctant to hear a friendship that had not worked out.

"I want to congratulate you on your new book. I have a copy on my coffee table. It is beautiful." She continued talking and then asked, "Is there anyone in your life?"

Dan was not sure what to say, because he simply did not know. His answer was short and to the point. "Maybe."

She accepted his answer without comment and they continued their dinner.

When it was time to go she said she would take the cabbie home by herself, but could they get together again soon. Dan agreed and said that he would call her.

Dan was through work early Friday afternoon. He called her and they decided to go sightseeing for the weekend. For three days they walked and talked and thoroughly enjoy each other's company. But after each evening dinner Caroline went to her home and Dan went to his hotel.

The next weekend was much the same.

Caroline had cared very much for Dan but they had drifted apart. There had never been any disagreements only space and time. But sharing this time with him she realized how much she had missed him. His demeanor was warm and she felt maybe he wanted to pick up where they left off a while back. She felt she wanted to give it another try. They had shared much and Caroline wanted that again.

After a candlelight dinner one evening Caroline boldly but tenderly asked him to go home with her. Of course Dan knew what she was asking. They had loved before and their relationship had been wonderful but things were different now. Both had contributed to their drifting apart.

Dan did not know what to say at first, although he knew what he thought. Finally he said as he took her hand, "Remember when you asked if there was anyone in my life and I said—maybe."

She knew instantly what he meant. "You'll go home and just like before, I won't see you for a long time and maybe never."

Again, the right words did not come. He simply shook his head in agreement.

"I met this girl at a reception in my old hometown. She absolutely captured my heart. Although when I left for here things had suddenly turned bad. That is where the maybe comes in."

Dan was so sad to say goodbye because he liked her very much. Time had not been right before and for sure it was not right now.

In his heart he felt sure Christina would find her way out of whatever was bothering her. If only I knew. He could not forget their first night together and how easily she had loved him. To himself he said, thank god for that storm. If it hadn't been she might not have offered me to stay.

Caroline said, "This was a beautiful evening, a farewell evening. It is nice to go out this way. At least our farewell is not angry." After a long pause she continued, "I don't want to lay myself bare but if she is not there when you get back, can we give it another try." Dan nodded his head yes and Caroline could see the sudden emotional distress in his face. It spoke loud.

She could not say a harsh word to him because he had been and was so nice to her. With a heavy heart he put her in a cab and she went off into the night.

♥

Dan had been in London thirty days and was scheduled to fly home the next day arriving late Friday night. Feeling sad he left London and Caroline behind. He felt sure he would never see her again, at least the relationship would not be the same.

He had not called Christina and had only written post cards with brief notes. But of course he had not mentioned Caroline. He planned to call Christina Saturday morning and drive out and be with her.

CHAPTER FOURTEEN

♥

The morning brought a misty rain that was so like fall, that lifeless time between the end and before a beginning, gray fall to winter white.

Saturday mornings were special for Christina and her papa. This was the one day they enjoyed breakfast together. They talked about the past week, school and papa whatever in retirement that had kept him busy. Although Chris did not tell him that she was going to tell Dan she wanted a break for a while. Her papa had sensed that something was still disturbing her, but did not ask what. He did ask her when Dan was to return and she abruptly said, she did not know.

While they were still lingering over coffee the phone rang. Quickly Chris said, "It's probably Dan.

I'll get it," and went into the library and closed the door.

It was Dan and he began, "Hi love."

Chris did not respond.

"I got back late last night and hopefully you have no plans for today. I want very much to see you."

Her voice was heavy but she said, "I'm glad you're home safe." She thought where do I begin. "Well, we left each other in sort of . . ."

He interrupted, "I do remember and I hope you feel better by now."

"Well I'm not sure I do. I believe it is going to take more than a month," she finally was able to say.

"I don't understand, is it me?"

"I'm not sure."

"Well, what are you not sure of," he said as his voice grew a little agitated.

"May I come out and we can talk. This relationship has a very deep meaning for me and I want it to go forward. We're not in high school. Either we go forward seriously or we have come to the end. I just don't understand, especially if you can't be specific."

"Well I can," she said abruptly, barely believing it was finally coming out.

"I have a heavy heart and it won't go away."

"It won't go away? What is *it*?" he asked. "Who has given you a heavy heart? Have I given you a heavy heart? Christina is there someone else in your life?" He knew she was distressed, but another man in her life. I just don't believe it. She must be using this as an excuse, his thoughts were wild.

"Sort of," and she began to cry.

"I don't want to hear this on the phone, I am coming out. Be there! I need an explanation! Have you been deceiving me?" His words were approaching erratic.

"No! No! But I can't see you just now," she pleaded.

"Listen Christina," he said strongly. "Please listen to me for a moment!" Then more calmly he said, "Whatever it is I want to hear it from you, and whatever it is I will accept. If you don't want me in your life and I know why, I will accept. But I have to know why!"

She was speechless.

"I'm leaving immediately. Be there!" He ended his conversation abruptly.

Dan quickly gathered clothes and personal items, if he needed to stay the night, and he was on his way.

Papa was still in the kitchen when Christina finished talking.

"Was that Dan?" he asked as he looked up and saw the distress in her face. She went into the living room and Papa followed.

"Oh darling, what's the matter?" he quickly asked. With her voice tight and stressed she told him everything, even more than she had told Dan.

"Oh, no–you didn't," he said as sorrow well up in his voice. "You can't go on like this."

"Papa, Brian just won't go away. I love Dan, but Brian can't be here too. What do I do?"

"Try, try, he's a good man. You both are lucky to find each other. Are you and Dan going to get married?"

"I don't know any more," she said pathetically.

"Oh Chris, how loud do I have to say, Brian is gone before you realize it. You can't see him, you can't touch him. It was a tragedy, but he died. It's over Chris, he's gone." Papa Zeller did raise his voice, something he almost never did, especially to Christina.

"I know," she said softly, "but . . ." she couldn't finish.

"I know you loved him, but that love has to be put away. Love is to be shared."

"I know," she said again, "but I want to be at peace with myself when I come to Dan."

"That love can never be fulfilled. You are here and he is not. I know grief and there is nothing easy about it. You have to work at it. You've had over two years and you are very young. Losing your mother, I could hardly stand it. It was the worst feeling I've ever had. Sometimes it was uncontrollable, but you can control how you handle it. You have to let him go." Papa paused and said to himself, oh god give me words.

"What you planned, it didn't happen, and now it can never happen. Dear child," and Papa went on. "Now and for always Brian *must*, be only a dream and must find his place of rest. Go with Dan, if you love him and if you don't, that's over too."

He tried to console her but she was so upset that his efforts seemed to be in vain.

An hour or more had passed and Christina seemed quieter and had been in deep contemplation.

"Papa, he said he's coming out." And she suddenly got up from her chair and left the room and she said to her papa, "Tell him I'll be back if I'm not here when he gets here."

Through her muffled voice and her turning away, papa did not completely hear what she had said. He thought, she'll tell me later.

She went to her room and got the little box that she had so treasured that held those golden curls. She knew the time had come. I promised Jan, I promised myself. It is over.

Back downstairs she said to her papa. "I'm leaving."

"No Chris, please don't," her papa pleaded with her.

Her emotions at last seemed to find reason. She grabbed her jacket and ran to her car. As she did she stopped briefly and picked a handful of red mums. She jumped into her car and drove quickly out of sight.

This time it was her papa who watched from the big window. My beautiful, beautiful child, wracked with so much pain and life has hardly begun for her, he thought. He felt so helpless. He shook his head in dismay. "I tried, I tired," he said out loud.

♥

A while later the dogs announced Dan's arrival. He carried himself quickly from his stopped car into her house. He did not even give Daisy and Henry any attention.

Papa Zeller welcomed him sadly.

Almost without greeting Dan asked, "Where is she? What went wrong? I had no idea there is someone else in her life. Why did she deceive me?" Confused and assuming papa knew everything, he asked again, "Where is she?"

"She isn't here," her father stated in his gentle and dignified voice. His voice contrasted with Dan's harsh questions.

"I'll go to her! Where is she?" he asked again, his voice firm. "Do you know what's happening? Give me something to deal with. I don't know where to start."

"Yes, I know. I'll tell you if you promise to be gentle and understanding. Offer her patients. I believe, now, she has reached or reaching a point when things are about to come to rest for her."

Dan could not imagine but he wanted to hear it from her and not her papa. "Oh, I will, I will."

"Go to Lake Road and turn south, drive about ten miles. I believe you will see her car off to the right." Papa's voice was full of sympathy as he notice how intent Dan listened without question. "You'll see, give her time son. I believe she wants and needs you. I know she loves you."

Without further question Dan turned and was gone. As her father watched again from the big window, Dan's car was quickly out of sight.

Dan had not questioned his destination. He did not care where she was, but his objective was to see her at least one last time. He drove with agitation and a bit too fast. As he turned south he started looking for her car. He came to his senses and thought of something besides seeing Christina. He finally questioned, where am I going? What will I say to her? How does one prepare for the unknown? He drove wildly on.

In the long flat stretch ahead he caught sight of a red car. It was hers. Dan stopped. He got out and looked around. Gray clouds hung lifeless in the smoke blue sky. The crisp air was motionless in the silent world around. Evergreens and ageless pines stood guard as they pointed toward eternity. A small stone wall surrounded the final resting place for many. The high–arched iron gateway held one word. **PEACE** And it was peace that came over Dan as he walked through the half–open gate.

At first he did not see her, because the tombstones and small evergreens blocked his view. But as he walked the tree–lined path, he caught sight of her alone in a far corner, just as her papa had said. There beneath a huge weeping willow ready for its long sleep of winter, she was sitting on the cold ground, knees bent and her face hidden in her crossed arms.

As Dan got closer she heard his footsteps on the wet leaves. She looked up briefly at him, thinking, oh no! I didn't want him to see me here. Didn't papa tell him?

Dan stopped short and read:

BRIAN JONATHAN KELLY
1945-1968

Dan stood silent. His whole being stopped. A chill came over him. He was not prepared for this, but in one brief moment he understood everything. All these months I've been competing with a dead man. His troubled thoughts, that had never stopped, asked, what do I do? Do I pick her up? Do I leave her here to grieve? Is this my one last visit? Should I intrude in these intimate moments with her and a death? He always seemed to have an answer in difficult situations, but now his wisdom failed him.

The world around was like the silence that death brings. The distant sounds had stopped somewhere in between. Overhead the dull lifeless sky offered nothing.

Finally Dan decided to face the reality that Christina had not. What can I lose he thought? He sat down on a stone near her. Softly he asked, "Chris do you love me, if you don't, I'll just leave and it will all be over."

To his surprise she quickly answered as she shook her head. Muffled, but very clear he heard. "Yes! Yes!"

Dan continued softly, "I respect your grief but it has been long over two years. And—there is a time to put these things away—You're young, you're here and you have a life to live." He continued as he pathetically grappled for words. "If you stay here, it is not solitude but a cold force. If you choose this empty world music will be without passion. There will be no exchange of love—no gentle words to hear—no soft touch from a hand—excitement will not be a sharing—sharing only a fantasy—sounds of laughter, children playing or spring will all be meaningless—

224

night will be silent and black. Alone will be all of these things if you choose to remain with . . . Life and its joys will be far away and that would belong to others—I have never been in love before so I don't know what it's like to love and to lose—but I too would eventually belong to someone else—let the past sleep because it's a long sleep—Christina I love you more than you can know and I want to marry you—be my wife—have our babies—I want to share this joyful life with you—it's decision time between a life—or a death."

Dan got up quickly and his last words were, "I'll wait for you at home." He stood for a moment and looked around in bewilderment. He noticed a fresh patch of earth on the grave.

He walked away leaving her to decide her and their fate. He wondered if he had said the right things, said too much, not enough.

Dan got into his car more perplexed than ever. His heart cried for her and he wondered if he had reached her. One part of that relationship had died and the other went on living, hoping and caring almost as if nothing had happened. Dan drove back to her home and Papa Zeller met him at the door.

"You found her?"

"Yes," Dan said faintly without emotion. "No words explained everything."

"Now you know why I asked you to be patient with her. I suppose she just had to go through whatever her heart demanded. She is a very strong girl but his death shattered her, so completely. It shattered all of us."

Her papa continued the story as they walked slowly to the library. He walked to the bay window and looked away as he continued as if Dan wasn't there. "His death, so sudden. One night late when he was going home from work, a deer ran in front of his car and he swerved and hit a tree. It was believed he died instantly. She was just finishing graduate school. It was over two years ago but there hasn't been any reason for her to forget him, so she just let him stay in her heart. Their friendship had been long—they were both fourteen. They were washing ponies at the stables when they met. She was never interested in anyone else, even in college. I don't believe he was either. Their friendship grew to love and they planned to be married. You're the only guy she has accepted a second date with in all this while. You'll never know how happy that made me because I felt all the past had come to an end and she was ready to start over."

Dan thinking should I know this? He is speaking as if I'm not here.

Papa Zeller went on almost unaware of Dan's presence. "We talked after you left last time. She told me that she never made love to him. Then I told her your love would be special for both of you, I hope she heard me."

Dan knew more or less that she had never made love to anyone else, but he could not believe how candidly her father was speaking.

Maybe it is more than I need to know, but at least I do understand, he thought as he gazed into the slow burning flame.

Papa Zeller continued, "It's what happened in her life. Certainly nothing she caused or could have prevented. Yet she had to face and accept it, but it seems she didn't. Your presence, your love has challenged her to bring this to an end. It should have happened long ago. Now it is playing out before you. This shouldn't have happened either. I hope after all this you'll still love her. I know she loves you and would be devastated all over again should you go. With you she'll be fine."

After another pause, "Henry was his dog. His mother said he should come and live with Chris and Daisy. He was grieving too. Being here would help and it did."

Papa Zeller turned to Dan, "Now you know almost everything. It will be easier for her. They were words she could not say to you."

No one spoke for a long time, just the crackling of the wood burning to a dusty end.

"I told her that I would wait for her here, after many words I told her that it was decision time. I have made it very clear that I love her and want to marry her. I believe I have loved her from the moment I saw her that summer evening and never looked back."

Dan and Papa Zeller had not realized how much time had passed.

♥

Christina sat on the cold ground in the vast silence surrounded by emptiness and abandon by life. The world around her was like the silence that death brings. Her thoughts were loud and strong. I do know he is gone. I know that he is lifeless and entombed. A final act that cannot be reversed. She knew she had come one last time to say goodbye and to do one last thing. She was fulfilling the promise that she had made to Jan and to herself. I can let go because I want life and Dan. I can go to him with peace in my heart.

She got up and walked quickly then stopped and turned and blew one last kiss, a tender and loving gesture that he would never know. "Goodbye," she whispered softly. "I would like to have shared life with you but death intervened. This goodbye must last for an eternity. I'll never be back." She turned and walked on as tears rolled down her face.

She too, was not aware how much time had passed. She ran from the cemetery, closed the gate behind and was quickly in her car. I must go to Dan. It can't be too late, was her dreadful thought.

As she drove toward her home the sun began to find its way through the distant clouds. As she came in sight of her big stone house a relief came over her. Dan's car was still there.

She ran onto the porch. The dogs had announced her coming so her papa went to the door. "He's in the library," he said. Throwing her jacket aside she ran quickly to him, closing the door behind.

Dan was standing in front of the fireplace, gazing deeply into the gentle flames that warmed the room. He turned easily and looked her way. His dark eyes offered only a look of uncertainty.

Chris was the first to speak. "Can you forgive me? I went to say goodbye and told Papa to tell you that I would be back. Did he?"

"No—Papa just told me where to find you. But if I wasn't supposed to be there then I will wipe it from my memory. I will never speak of it again."

"I had nothing else to cling to until I met you. I do want to marry you, oh—so—much. I love you—can you forgive me?" she asked again as her heart beat wildly for fear that it was too late to go forward with Dan. These few seconds seemed like forever as she waited for his answer.

Dan listened patiently and his stern expression slowly gave way to one of love and understanding. He walked slowly to her and took her in his arms.

"Oh my darling, the anguish you have been through. Forgive, what is there to forgive? Loving is a beautiful natural human emotion. So is grieving."

They held each other close for many moments.

Looking into her soft brown eyes, "Love is ours now. Are you at peace with yourself?"

"Oh Dan love, yes. I found peace that evening at Bellamy House. You were so satisfying to watch. There was a contentment that came over me. I went to bed that night and your arms were around me. Through all of our upsets along the way, I loved you and you have brought peace to my heart. I'm so sorry," and he hushed her words with his finger tip.

"There is nothing to be sorry for," and he paused. "That night after the reception I just could not get you out of my mind and I too took you to bed with me."

He took her face in his hands and softly said, "And it's just too bad that we didn't get to enjoy it together."

And she smiled ever so warmly at him.

"Christina love, if you are at peace, I'm at peace."

She responded, "Yes so very much."

"Will you marry me?" he simply asked.

"Oh yes! Oh yes! I'm so very sure that I love you with my whole being, my body, my heart, my soul unconditionally, all of me," she said so very softly as tears well up in her eyes and streamed slowly down her face.

"Oh my love, we'll be great together. All my life I've searched for you. Others just would not do. My life is too important to me to give it away frivolously. Life is beautiful and must be used in a beautiful way. I knew from the moment I saw you that somehow you would be everything that I had hoped for and you are and so much more," he said as he kiss the tears on her face.

"Sit down love," he softly asked of her. In front of her he knelt down on one knee.

He took both her hands, "I was going to write beautiful words for this moment but I will just ask you, will you marry me, be my wife and forever be my lover." And he smiled as he looked into those eyes that touched his soul.

"Oh I will, oh yes I will. I want to be all those things to you and for you always."

"But I am prepared otherwise." He reaches in his pocket and pulled out a tiny blue velvet covered box.

"I've been carrying this around for a while. He opened it and took out a ring that held a very large and sparkling diamond. He looked lovingly into those eyes and as he slipped it on her finger he said, "And this is only a symbol of my love for you. The real love is in my heart."

They rose and lingered in each other's arms for a very long time and finally Dan said, "I don't want to leave you here. Come home with me tonight and tomorrow we'll come back and we can announce this to the world."

Christina was so filled with emotion and happiness she could hardly speak, "I don't know how I could have ever doubted you. I believe I knew too from that first moment I saw you, but it was a surprise and I did not know how to handle my emotions. You have made me very happy in every way possible. Your love, your kindness, all wrapped up in such a beautiful body. A soul filled with all the beautiful things of life. I know with you there will always be happiness. Let's go tell Papa."

They found Papa Zeller still gazing out the window. As they approached he was not sure what they were about to say, neither carried a telling expression.

"Papa," Chris asked, "are you all right."

"Yes, are you guys?"

With that she held out her hand to show papa the ring that Dan had just placed on her finger.

He simply took her hand and kissed it as tears rolled down his cheek. "I'm so happy for both of you. Beautiful child you found your way with this wonderful man. Somehow I knew you would."

Christina wiped the tears from his cheek.

"John," Dan began. "I know this is a little backward but sometimes things happen this way. But I ask for your daughter's hand in marriage. I'll love and cherish her everyday more than the one before and until the last breath in my body."

"Son you have my blessing and her mother sends a blessing also. I welcome you to this family and now it is complete."

"Papa we're going back to the city tonight and we'll be back tomorrow and announce this to the world," as she looked lovingly at Dan.

"Honey, if you want to be together you don't have to go back to the city. It is getting late. You love each other, you should be together. Being together is natural. Don't miss a day. If only I could just be with your mother one more time. We didn't miss much in our life. We loved each other often. And I miss her so much—so much. The little things and the big. And yet I don't want to be selfish. We had many years together and five beautiful children." He paused, "Unless you have to leave, but know that you don't have to. You can sleep here in each other's arms tonight and any other night you choose. This is your home, Christina, Dan."

"Oh Papa, you have so much love. And that is why I love you," she said as she hugged him.

She looked at Dan and her expression was asking. What do you want to do?

She asked. "Dan doesn't have clothes for tomorrow?"

"Yes, Dan has clothes. I came prepared to stay, at the hotel if need be." And he shook his head in a yes. "If you want," as he looked at her.

"We'll stay Papa."

Papa said, "That's good it's a long drive to the city and you must be tired from your long flight. I told Ellen I would watch a movie with her tonight. I had better call and tell her I'll be over. Can I tell her the good news?"

They both said, "Yes."

Papa went to Ellen's for the remainder of the evening.

Chris and Dan went into the library and were just together for a long while.

"It is not too late to have dinner out. If you would like."

"I think we deserve it."

"Where is the closest romantic place," he asked her.

She thought for a moment, "I know, Alexander's."

Dan asked, "How long will it take to drive there?"

"About fifteen minutes," she replied.

"I'll call and see if they can accommodate us."

He called and they said they could, in an hour.

Dan got his things from his car and they went to Christina's bedroom which would now be their bedroom. They dressed and were on their way to dine.

It had been a very emotional day for both, but they knew it was an end and also a beginning of their life together.

At dinner they relaxed and showed their devotion to each other. An aura of love surrounded them and it was obvious they were thinking of the present and had put the past away.

They got home late and Dan put his car in the back garage. Papa was not home yet so Christina put the little light on that would guide him up the drive to home. They went to their bedroom. They showered together and free of all nightly attire they fell asleep in each other's arms. They slept so soundly they did not even hear papa come home.

♥

Morning and the sun was yet hidden behind the horizon. Chris was awake but she did not want to move for she did not want to wake Dan. But somehow he sensed and said, "Good morning to my loving wife, Mrs. Halloran."

She rolled over and faced him, "And to my beautiful husband, good morning too."

"I would like to be more original but this is truly the first day of the rest of our lives," he said as he pushed her hair back and caressed her face.

"Oh yes," as she softly touched his face and around his mouth. He rolled over on his back and pulled her on top of him and wrapped his arms around her. She laid her head on his shoulder and said, "You know what married people do."

"Let's," and with that he closed his eyes and found her waiting lips that he parted with his fingertips. They caressed each other's bodies with tenderness and care until their desires could not wait. He said softly, "I want to do this every time as if it would be the last. I want to love you every time as if it was the first." And they truly became one.

♥

Although Papa got home late he was awake early and took care of the dogs and fixed breakfast for them and then disappeared to the library. He did not call Chris and Dan but let them be at peace. He knew all too well what love was all about. He and Lydia did lots of things before and after marriage. He just didn't talk about it.

Chris and Dan finally got up, showered, dressed and ready for a day of announcing the happy news to family and to friends. They both stopped to say good morning to papa and he told them their breakfast was ready.

At breakfast Chris asked, "Before we start calling to tell everybody, should we have a date in mind."

Dan's answer was, "Soon."

She smiled, "I like soon."

"You mentioned your brothers are all going to be here for Christmas. Would that be enough time to plan?" Dan asked.

"I suppose, that with a lot of intense planning that could be done. Maybe we should try because John and Rachel are so far away. I want all my brothers here. Your brother doesn't live that far and your mother and dad are just a couple hours away."

"Did you want a big wedding?" Dan asked.

"Well, I haven't given it much thought. Although I think it would be nice to have a small gathering of close family and then a big reception."

"What about here in your beautiful home—the library, the living room. Both are warm and elegant and spacious," Dan added.

"Papa would be so proud that we selected his home to start our home."

Dan smiled, "That was easy and a wonderful plan. Our wedding here at Christmas. Christmas day, early afternoon and then a big reception somewhere close."

"My family will all be here to help. I'm excited already," Chris said.

Dan pulled her hand to his lips and kissed her palm.

"Let's tell your papa," they did and yes he was so pleased that they had decided to be married here, as Christina knew he would.

Chris and Dan waited a while and then started their many phone calls. First his mother and father, his brother. Her brothers Dave and Jim who live near each other. Bill earlier and John last. They told them all that it would be a Christmas wedding and further details would be forthcoming. And yes Christina called her friend and confident Jan. She squealed with delight. "I knew you would find your way. Can I call anyone at school?" Chris said yes. "Are you going to be there tomorrow?"

"Yes."

"I'll see you then, love you Chris."

"Love you too Jan."

"I just checked my schedule and I knew it was late, but I don't have to be in the studio until one o'clock tomorrow," Dan reported. "We're filming a couple interviews for the symphony booklet."

"Go to school with me tomorrow morning and you can leave from there. I don't believe anyone other than Jan even knows we have been seeing each other. This is going to be a shock."

"I can do that."

It was a busy, busy, happy, happy day at the Zeller residence with just the three, but then Ellen came over.

After everything quieted down, Ellen and Christina prepared dinner in the evening. It was a little family that was growing again.

♥

Chris and Dan got up early the next day and got ready to leave. Chris told Dan she would ride to school with him and Jan would bring her home. If she can't papa will come in.

They got to school and hour before it started. They went to the teacher's room and almost everybody was there. The room had been decorated. The word truly had spread far and fast. They had only expected to see Christina but to their delight her beloved had accompanied her on this first day to share in the announcement.

Jan greeted Chris and they hugged as best friends do and she told her how happy she was for her and that everything had worked out as they both had hoped. Christina introduced her to Dan and in his gracious manner he kissed her on the cheek and expressed his delight to know her.

Many knew Dan from his career accomplishments and they were excited to meet him. Most of all, their engagement was a hugh surprise, because no one but Jan knew that she had been seeing him, much less soon to marry one of the most eligible and desirable men around.

Dan and Chris thanked everyone for the warm welcome and the thoughtfulness on such short notice. And he announced there would be a Christmas wedding.

They moved into the hall as Dan was getting ready to leave and classes were about to start. The students were all excited too, especially those that were attending her classes. The word spread fast. Ms. Zeller got engaged to Mr. Halloran.

"Mr. Halloran do you remember us. It was me and Zack that were talking to her when you came over at the reception."

"I do and I'm so glad you shared her with me," he replied.

They both chatted with students and teachers introduced themselves to Dan.

Dan said to Chris, "I'll be going and will call this evening, probably late," and he kissed her on the lips. A big cheer rose from the students. They both were a little surprised but smiled.

He was off and classes started and it took a while for everybody to settle down.

Christina didn't do much teaching, the students wanted to know about Dan and his work.

The day went fast and Jan drove her home and she stayed for dinner. The white florist van had visited again. It came before Chris was home from school so papa received the eleven roses, six buds and five fully opened. He did not read the card. He would do that later. Christina must be first.

She told Jan they planned a Christmas wedding here at home and she asked her to be her maid of honor. Tears welled up in Jan eyes. "Nothing would make me happier."

"This had been a long road for you to happiness. But you have found the best. And you certainly deserve each other. Oh Chris! He is beautiful."

"I tell him that all the time," she said. "He told me to stop a long time ago, but I haven't yet."

They continued to talk and Chris told her about Saturday. What was supposed to happen but didn't and how loving and understanding Dan had been about it all.

"He is a perfect gentleman," Jan acknowledged.

And so the turmoil that love presented them had finally been satisfied and Christina settled down and began serious plans for their special day.

CHAPTER FIFTEEN

♥

November. The beauty of fall had ceased to be. Vibrant colors and harvest had surrendered. The lands were bare and revealing. Trees are stark and naked. The evergreens darkened for their sleep. Red berries rest exposed on the bare branches. The brisk winds and sharp raindrops are being replaced slowly by winter white that will become pure and fresh. This was the world that Daniel and Christina began their life together.

Christina at last found the happiness that she thought had passed her by. For Daniel, he found the happiness that he had never known. He walked into her life that summer evening and never looked back. They walked forward together. Christina stumbled and almost fell. Dan caught her and cradled her and held her, as not to fall again. He gave her confidence, strength and love of himself. He held them together with his love and understanding. An understanding she came to know and went to him with her heart at peace. They would bring their new love to share with each other and now become one. It was truly after sunset.

♥

It was the middle of the month and plans must start immediately. Christina spent all week making arrangements, so when she saw Dan next weekend she would have tentative plans and then they could together finalize their special day. Reception and where, invitations, how many people, music, dress, all the things that had to be put in place and now. She was going to the big city Friday after school. Dan assured her that he would be home to meet her.

But this week she wanted to visit Brian's mother and tell her that she was going to be married. She had visited her frequently but not so much since Dan had occupied her life.

She called Evelyn and they made arrangements and yes, she would have dinner with her. Her daughter was married so she lived alone. It would be bittersweet after such a day as last Saturday. Christina had one last thing to do to put Brian's memories to rest.

Christina arrived and she was warmly greeted. Evelyn immediately congratulated her.

"Oh no," Chris said. "I came to tell you. It only happened last Saturday."

"Come on in and we'll have a glass of wine before dinner."

"How did you hear?"

"A friend of mine has a friend that works in the cafeteria at school. She told me about the excitement. She saw Dan and thought he was very handsome."

Chris laughed, "I tell him he's beautiful. But he really is a beautiful man, inside and out."

"I'm not sure why I remember, but the reception last summer at Belamy House, there was a write-up in the newspaper."

"Yes, that is where I met him. In a gentle and determined way, he was unrelenting from that moment on. It caught me by surprise. At that time I hadn't let Brian go."

"I was afraid that you hadn't, but I'm glad to know you overcame the loss we both shared. There has been enough time," Evelyn responded lovingly.

They talked about what she had been doing in retirement, her daughter and her two grandchildren.

But they came back to the one they shared in love, Brian.

"I remember I always knew where he was. He was very fond of your mother and the way she would sit with you two and go over your literature classes. And so many times you brought him home."

Chris added, "When mother died he was there for me. Papa was so shocked and distraught and it was hard to reach him for a while, but Brian was there helping me through."

"How is your father?"

"He's very good. He does some consulting. He checks on the new horses at the Grange or Benton's. He enjoys his flower gardens. He says he didn't have time for such luxury when working and raising kids. He went to San Francisco to visit John in September. All he could talk about was the girls and how they pampered him."

"Your parents were an important part of his growing up to be a good man. Losing his father at that age is a terrible thing for a boy. I had to be away at work all too much, I didn't have a choice."

"He would tell me about what he and your father talked about those many nights that he brought him home. They made an impression on him and you'll never know how I appreciated all your father and mother did for him. Only to lose him," Evelyn said as her eyes became full.

"Evelyn please know he often told me how much he loved you and his father."

"He was a loving child."

"He was a loving man."

"Where are you going to live?" Evelyn asked changing the subject.

"For now in Chicago. Dan works out of there."

"I would like for you to come to the reception. Dan knows everything and he will be very gracious. We're having our wedding at our home and just for the family. The reception probably at the Le Chateau."

"No. No. I couldn't be happier for you but it is your time with friends and family. I'm part of the past. I'll pray for you and Dan to have a long and happy life and many children."

They spent a wonderful evening as they had so many times before.

Finally Chris said, "There is one more thing I have to do. When I met Brian and from that very day until I lost him, I kept a diary about the two of us. I hoped to read it to him one day and we surely would laugh."

She paused and then continued. "It was our growing up together, our closeness, our separations, what we said to each other. A very vivid ten years. My last entry was about my painting that I called After Sunset. I wrote a love letter to him. My tears fell on the page as I was writing. I closed it and have never opened it. I want you to have it. It is part of the past that I can't keep. I know if I do, I'll read it someday and grieve again. And I don't want to do that. It isn't fair to me or to Dan, because I do passionately love him."

She paused as her breath caught.

"I'm not obliterating Brian from my memory, nor can I, nor do I want to, but he has found the corner of my heart where he will rest undisturbed. I'm at peace with him and as the years pass that peace will grow stronger. And I want you to have this. Read it if you want to or not. It will be some of those ten years that you never knew." With that Chris handed her diary to Evelyn.

"Oh my gosh, I didn't know," otherwise Evelyn could not speak. She put her hands to her mouth and closed her eyes to hold back the tears.

Christina said goodbye to her, "Until next time, do take care of yourself. I love you Brian's mother."

It was late when Christina drove home and she went right to bed. She was truly at peace with her past. She felt proud of herself because she did not cry. Just almost.

♥

Friday came at last and classes were over. Jan stopped by quickly to wish her well on this visit to the city. She was thinking of the last one and how bad it had turned out. This one will be different. They hugged and, "See you Monday."

Christina had gathered information that she and Dan would discuss and make decisions about. She arrived just as it was getting dark and she was glad of that. Dan saw her arrive and went to the car to help her with her bag. First he kissed her quickly on the lips. When inside they embraced tenderly.

"I hope it's always like this."

"For me it will be."

"I'm so relieved you're here. I didn't want you driving around after dark. And this time you got to park right in front of the house."

"Everything went well. I got out of school just at three. Jan gave me a good send off."

Inside he helped her with her coat and said "Come I'll show you around. It will take all of three minutes. But I suppose we'll live here for a while until we can find a larger place. Although I've been looking for a two bedroom in the area. My lease is until April. I want to get one soon. Your papa will want to come up. Mom and Dad will too."

Dan gave her a quick tour and it did only last a few minutes. Chris thought it was nice but small, but it was only Dan by himself.

245

"We do have a lot to talk about, our wedding, Thanksgiving, Christmas. Oh my gosh, it's overwhelming," she said but laughed. "We can do it. We'll probably have many more dilemmas over the years."

"Yeah, we'll tackle them all with zest. Nothing too big that we can't handle, but tonight I'm going to take you out to dinner. You deserve it. You have been cooking for me a lot lately. So it's on me tonight. I made reservations for seven–thirty at the little French place. It's very nice, cozy, and they have wonderful food. It's close and we can walk. You probably want to freshen up or a shower."

"It is so cold out. I need to get warm. A nice hot shower would be nice only if you were with me," she said as she gazed into his eyes.

"I left myself open for that," as he playfully took her in his arms. "Let's. I haven't been home long and I too need to be refreshed. We couldn't start our weekend any better."

The shower was warm and comforting, but the pleasures they each received and gave were tender and caring, sending a message of excitement.

They rested for a while and Dan suggested they dress and be on their way to dinner.

They dressed in front of each other without the least bit of shyness. He buttoned her wool dress. She buttoned his shirt. Chris started to brush her hair and Dan asked, "May I do that for you?"

Oh yes, Chris thought as she handed him her brush. It always feels better when someone else does it.

Dan sat down on the corner of the bed and said to her "Sit here," as he spread his legs and there he brushed her hair and rubbed her neck with the other hand.

"Your hair always smells so good. I'll have to use your shampoo . . . earrings. I designated that as my job."

And again he put her earring in for her. His warm hands gently touched her ears as he did the task perfectly. Even though they had just made love she felt an overwhelming desire to begin again.

"Dan, we had better go before we get delayed again."

He smiled, "That wouldn't be bad at all. But you're right. We have the whole weekend."

With that they put on their heavy coats, gloves and Chris her hat and they were on their way.

She tucked her arm in his and he took her hand and they walked briskly to the restaurant. They both agreed it was turning to winter fast.

The restaurant was only about four blocks, or so.

They lingered a long while with wine before ordering dinner. Of course they were discussing their wedding plans. They also talked about school and Dan's latest assignment. He also told her that he would take her to dinner tomorrow, but he had bought breakfast things and that he would prepare it for her.

They walked home more slowly. It was a busy area with small boutiques and restaurants.

At home they had a cup of tea in Dan's small kitchen nook. It had been a long week for both and the walk to and from the restaurant and all the other amenities, they were very tired. Although . . .

♥

"Good morning," he said as he found her near him under the down comforter.

"Hi there," she said and rolled to her side and faced him.

"I'm so glad I have this big bed. At first I thought I'd get a smaller one. Then I thought this better."

"You're so smooth and soft," he said as he ran his hand down the side of her body and her back.

"You don't exactly feel like a man of labor."

And she closed her eyes and enjoyed the moments. And that is how it began . . . again.

Exhausted, Dan went to make coffee. Chris followed.

She laughed, "I brought a robe when I came to visit you."

He looked at her, "Good thing because I don't have a closet full of extras. But I wouldn't care if you didn't have a robe and it was your idea that I stay. I always travel light."

They giggled, hugged and were playful.

They decided to go shopping because it was too cold for outside activities. They drove to one of the biggest malls and they began their shopping adventure. Christina bought things for her honeymoon. Dan had told her he was taking her to a warm environment. Otherwise, she agreed, it would be a surprise.

She didn't mind that Dan was there and he even picked out some delicate things. His heart leaped when he imagined her wearing them.

He is so gracious and so comfortable with himself, Christina thought.

They continued their shopping and Dan bought her some more things and a scarf that he thought would look nice with her white cashmere sweater.

He asked her, "What about your dress?"

"I'm going to wear my mother's wedding dress. I got it out this week and it is beautiful even after all these years. I'm just a little taller and thinner so I'll have it adjusted. But otherwise it will be perfect."

"You're a perfect size for me. I'm not the smallest guy around. I can cradle you and you can get lost in my arms. We have been so busy falling in love we haven't talked about children yet. Any thoughts."

Slowly Chris answered, "We'll let that come naturally. Now I need your answer to your question."

"I'm in agreement."

"Don't rush, we're not even married. We have another month," she said as she laughed.

He said looking tenderly at her, "Yes we'll get married first. I want us to just enjoy each other for a while without anything in the way. We have missed a lot of years together because we just met. We're young enough to start our family, next year."

As they walked along in the mall she looked at him and said, "I love you Dan Halloran . . . so very much."

"Yes, oh yes," he quietly answered as he gazed lovingly at her.

They spent the day just shopping and looking around, bookstores, music shops and boutiques.

Then they decided to go home relax and Dan had planned dinner at the Yea Old Tavern. They would have to drive but it wasn't far.

At home Dan asked her if she would like to go to Cathedral tomorrow for the musical hour and he also would show her some of his work. He only had a few, most were at his mother's. They relaxed a while and then decided to get ready for dinner. Their walking had given them a good appetite.

Chris put on her white cashmere sweater and Dan asked, "Where is your new scarf?"

"I'll get it."

"Earrings too."

She handed him both.

"The scarf, like this and let a bit hanging to the side. The earrings, one here and the other here," and the both laughed.

"You're so very good at these small things." And most of all she thought how gentle he is and sensuous he makes me feel.

"It's all part of photography 101," and they both laughed again.

She thought I'm so lucky to have found him, or rather he found me. And wouldn't give up. I love him so.

They both smiled very contentedly at each other.

"Let's be on our way, I'm getting hungry."

Driving there he told her where they were going and that he had never been there, but some of his colleagues had praised it.

"It can be a first for us," he said.

"We have had a lot of firsts," he smiled and reached for her hand.

An important first, Dan thought, she certainly is my first love. I know she once loved someone else, but I hope that someday she will think of me as her first true love. What matters now that we are passionately in love and soon to be married. Dan let his thoughts rest.

At dinner while enjoying a glass of wine Chris told Dan, "We checked at the Chateau about the reception. Papa insisted that he go with me and he would be taking care of all the cost. I was his only daughter. How well I know that. They can accommodate a large group and have a suite for our families. It is very elegant and they had a wonderful menu. They had several bands that would be available for dancing should we choose them.

Dan asked, "How close is it?"

"About fifteen minutes."

"And don't forget the bridal suite."

Her smile was one of love and contentment.

"I did get another, but I like the Chateau. Look and see what you like. I also have sample invitations for the reception. Monday after school I will finalize what we choose."

Driving home Chris said," Tomorrow call your parents and see if they will come for Thanksgiving. I also want to see some of your work."

Dan mentioned brunch. The Cathedral. And a few hugs and kisses.

It had been a long and busy day so they decided to retire and get an early start tomorrow.

♥

Morning and it was a bright sunny November day although the air was crisp. Dan got up and made coffee and then went back to bed with Christina. They shared a warm and intimate time to start this day. Coffee and a few other things for breakfast and they were ready to begin.

They walked to the Cathedral for the musical hour. The church was beautiful with its stained glass windows representing stories from the Bible. Chris and Dan sat holding hands and love flowed between them, holding this hour hostage in their hearts.

As they left Dan asked her how she liked that kind of service.

"It was really different as a spiritual service. It was more moving than if someone had given a sermon."

"My dear what you just said was music over words."

"I did didn't I. At times they are one of the same as they appeal to our emotions. You can cry, you can laugh, even be indifferent. And I have a perfect quote, 'Music is love in search of a word'. How's that for getting me out of a spot." And she laughed.

"Very good answer and a nice quote. What did you like best today?"

"I liked the vocal and piano best and the piano was like a mini recital. And you?"

"The string quartet. Brahms is always a favorite of mine."

"Did you take piano lessons?"

"No but often I wish that I had. I don't know how mother let that get away. But we always had music at home."

"There would always be time for lessons," Dan assured her.

"I know, but adult life gets in the way. I paint and have my literature and now I have the best of all—you," and she smiled.

"We'll remember the piano lessons when we have our little girls," she added.

"I hope we have a bunch of little girls, you deserve them. You have grown up with boys and now me, it's time for girls."

"That would be nice but first I want them healthy."

"Absolutely."

They walked on a few blocks when Dan said, "In the next block there is a Sunday brunch that is very good. Are you up to it?"

"Yeah, but I have eaten enough this weekend for the whole week. Now is not the time to gain weight."

"At brunch you can choose. Also this is lunch and dinner."

After enjoying all the different food, they walked home. First Dan called his parents and yes they would come for Thanksgiving. They would inform Jake the big dinner would be at the Zeller's instead of the Halloran's.

They took a last look at invitations for the wedding reception and decided on the other things that Christina would take home with her and finalize the plans

Then he got out a large folio of photos that he had taken in many different places. They included the last ones he had taken at her home, of her, their walk in the fog and of course the dogs. There were many black and white, some color, and collections having a theme. She especially liked the black and whites. Christina was totally enthralled and thought his approach to a subject was certainly unique. That is why he had become well known in his field.

"These black and whites are so beautiful. You certainly have a special touch. I can't wait to hang some of these in our home."

"Oh thank you. It's better when I can put a lot of thought into taking a photo. Some you have to grab quickly and then you have to see what happens."

As they talked, enjoying his photos, Dan highlighted the time with music. The next hour or so was playful, happiness and there was laughter.

"And I wasn't going to tell you until all was final but I'm pretty sure I'll have an assignment in Paris in April for a month. And of course you are going with me. That is the only way I'll accept long assignments. I just couldn't keep such a great secret."

Christina's eyes lit up, "Really! I'd love that. Dear heart you have brought love to my life and now Paris. When will you know?"

"It will be spring there and we'll know when we come back from our honeymoon and maybe before. It's rather final they're just talking price."

"Oh my, it just keeps getting better and better and what will you be doing."

"A French fashion magazine, I forget the name, is doing a ten page fashion spread and they requested that I do the photographing. I don't know how the filming schedule is going to be, but I think Kate will have it before we leave. If we don't have time while filming we'll stay a few extra days to take in some sights. Mont–St–Michelle, Versailles, whatever. It will be an extension of our honeymoon. But then again I want to make life an extension of our honeymoon."

"What a way to celebrate our days together," she responded.

Dan could see that it struck a happy chord with Christina. It's made me pretty happy too, he thought.

"I don't want to get too far ahead of myself, but give it some thought, maybe we can do a book together, something different. Something with art, literature. France is filled with artist and good writer, as you know. When things get finalized I'll go talk to my editor and get his take."

"While you're working I can take in all the museums. I'll brush up on my French. I took three years in high school. But that was a while ago."

"Great, you can teach me some. I took Spanish."

"You have a passport?"

'Yes, mother and I went to London with papa when, I guess, seventeen. I'll have to get a new one next year. She went with him when she could, but that was my first overseas trip. They were so devoted to each other."

"It's so wonderful and I want our life together to be just that way too."

"Have you given any thought what you want to do after were married?"

"No there hasn't been time. Although I applied for my leave of absence. You only resign if you are positive you will never be back to teach. This way I can sub and return to work at a later date if I so choose and there is an opening."

"That is good. You can reapply in the city or be substitute if you want to. How long does that last?"

"They give you five years leave. This is nice if you want to stay home with young children. What is your schedule like until Christmas?"

"My schedule until Christmas."

Dan reached in his wallet and checked to be accurate. "I have November twenty–fourth until Sunday. Then Saturday the eighteenth until we come back from our honeymoon."

"You will be out on weekends," she asked

"Yes, all of them. Hopefully no extra work will be necessary."

"We still have to finish our plans. Visit the florist, get our wedding bands, menu for Christmas Eve dinner."

"You plan and I'll be there."

"Have you finished your Christmas shopping?" she asked.

"Some of it. Maybe you can help me with the rest."

Then he said to her, "I want you to get started and out of the city before it gets dark. You'll call the moment you get home."

"The moment I get home."

She put her arms around him and his face fell into her soft brown hair, she said, "I don't want to go. You have made everything so special. I'll be glad when we won't have these separations."

"Oh sweetheart, to have you near always."

He picked her up and carried her to his bedroom. The door partially open and the music was flowing all around. Whisper of tones light and soft play upon each . . . a gentle weaving of harp strings gliding around only to meet again then part . . . a quick skip of a grace note . . . a melody in the bottom range only to find the melody soon at the top . . . the sounds meet in close harmony . . . one note joining another to make a chord . . . holding of low tones as the highs danced delicately around them in play . . . the rise of middle tones meeting and singing with pleasure . . . the strength of all the sounds swelling . . . then resolve into one long note to slowly and quietly reach a satisfying end.

CHAPTER SIXTEEN

♥

Thanksgiving was upon the land. Papa and Ellen shopped for all of the food for this bountiful holiday. Jan came out Wednesday after school and would be staying the night. Dan arrived later in the evening and he was very tired for he had worked from seven in the morning until late at night all week. A short week but it had been busy for everyone.

Very early the next day Christina helped Papa get the turkey in the oven. She then slipped quietly back into bed with Dan, so as not to wake him.

Soon Ellen arrived with pumpkin pies and a raspberry cake. She was a good cook even though she never had anyone in particular to express her cooking skills for, although she often prepared dinner for Papa Zeller.

Christina woke a little later and went for coffee. She heard Jan in the guest room and she stopped and knocked, "Can I come in?"

"Sure, I was just waking up. It's so peaceful to sleep here."

"As I told Dan wait till we all get here it won't be so peaceful. I was on my way for coffee, want some."

"Oh yeah, I can't do much till I have that first cup."

"I'm getting some for Dan and me."

Chris went for coffee to give all three of them a start for the big day.

She and Dan had their coffee and dressed. Ellen had made French toast and prepared a bowl of fruit.

After breakfast everyone was truly ready for the day.

Jan, Chris and Dan prepared the table with fall colored earthenware. Dan had ordered a mixed fall bouquet for a centerpiece. Christina had made little turkey place cards. Papa would be at the head of the table and Dan would be at the other "head" and she would be next to him.

The turkey was near done and the other food was also ready, it was a moment of relaxation.

Soon the dogs sensed a car in the drive, Daisy ran to the front window and looked out.

"Dan your folks are here. We're not expecting anyone else."

Dan and Chris put on their jackets and went out to meet them, as always accompanied by Daisy and Henry.

Hugs and introductions, Dan said to his brother Jake, "I'm so glad you could be here before the wedding and meet my girl. She met mom and dad last summer and they approved." He smiled at Chris and raised his brow. She winked back with a smile.

"You got here in good time," Dan said to Jake.

"We drove down and stayed at moms last night."

"That was a good idea."

Dan said to his nephews, "You can run with these guys," and pointed to the dogs. "Also there is a pool table in the rec room, and a television. You don't have to sit with us adults all the time." Dan knew what a thirteen and fourteen year old would rather do.

"Come on in," and Dan led the way with his father, brother and nephews. The girls followed slowly as they were in deep conversation about the ride, the country home and a few others things that had caught their attention.

Inside there were more introductions and everyone relaxed in the spacious living room.

Chris and Dan served appetizers and cocktails. Dan's father and Papa Zeller had a great conversation about the city, its growth and many other things that interest men. Dan's father remembered many things even though his company had him here for only a short time.

After much conversation and laughter and getting to know each other, Christina decided that it was time to enjoy all the good food awaiting them.

The girls got the food on the table and Papa was called to carve the turkey. Dan poured the wine. Everybody gathered at the table where Papa Zeller said a few words of thanks and expressed how happy he was to meet and be with his new family. And he offered a welcome toast.

After dinner everyone relaxed with coffee and more conversation. Dan's nephews too seemed to enjoy the day. They did all the things their Uncle Dan had suggested.

The day passed all too quickly. This was Dan and Christina's first family gathering, the first of many.

Everyone left for their homes and only Dan, Chris, Papa and Ellen remained. They chatted for a while and then Ellen too made her way home and papa retired for the night.

Dan and Chris snuggled in front of the fire in the library, just being together after the hectic holiday.

"Let me give you a foot massage."

"Oh yes."

"This was such a nice day, good food and company," Dan said as he counted eleven, a big bunch."

"Oh wait till you see all of us here."

"Did your mother have help when you were growing up?"

"Always. Papa provided her with somebody all the time. But we all had to keep our rooms clean."

"Today went well."

"It did. I try to plan well and Ellen helps me to get things done. But for Christmas Eve gathering I am going to hire two ladies from Blake's catering to prepare dinner. I want it to be more formal and I don't want anyone to have to cook. Blake's have helped us in the past. They are good."

"You tell them what you want prepared."

"I plan the menu and buy the food and they prepare. That way you know exactly what you are getting."

"You really take charge in a very natural way."

"I always helped mother and being a teacher helps," and she smiled at him and he returned by kissing her lovingly.

All the while they were talking he continued the gentle massage and Chris didn't miss a touch.

"That feels so good."

"We're the only ones left. Shall we, where we'll be more comfortable."

♥

The next two day Chris and Dan decorated for the Christmas holiday. It was a little early but Dan would be here to help her get everything out and get it into place. They put a big tree in the living room, all with Victorian ornaments. There were many to choose from, even from her grandmother's collection. They also put another big tree in the cellar recreation room for the little children and it was filled with toy ornaments. It would be where Santa would leave their presents. They also prepared many small vignettes for every room, even the bathrooms. Spending this time together gave them a warm feeling about family. They would decorate many times in the future, but this was their first.

♥

The weekends and the weeks passed and finally Christmas week had arrived. Christina had said goodbye to all her colleagues and would see them at the reception.

Dan had arrived Saturday with everything he needed until after their honeymoon. He would stay with Christina until after Christmas Eve festivities were over. They were going to observe the tradition of not seeing each other before the ceremony. Although Christina would have liked Dan to be there and take pictures of the little ones on Christmas morning, but tradition is tradition.

Monday the San Francisco Zellers arrived and were met at the airport by Dan, Chris and Papa. Before introductions could begin, Julie and Katie ran to papa who waited with open arms.

"Papa, Julie and me are going to come and spend the summer with you." She whispered in his ear, "We haven't told dad yet."

John and Rachel were surprised and had puzzling smiles for each other.

"That would be the greatest but you have to get approval from mother and dad."

"We hope it snows while were here, a lot," Katie said in her energetic way." As John watched he thought so often she reminds me of Christina at every age.

Although it wasn't necessary, Chris said to John and Rachel, "This is my Dan."

John with both hands, "I am overjoyed to know you and welcome." Rachel too expressed delight to meet him.

Finally the girls gave Aunt Christina a big hug and she said to Dan, "This is Julie and Katie, two of my favorite nieces."

Dan graciously shook hands with both of them and said, "I'm so very glad to meet both of you young ladies and glad you are here."

"We are too Uncle Dan," Katie speaking for both.

John hugged Chris and whispered in her ear, "I love you baby sister and you'll never know how happy I am for you and Dan."

"Thank you, all this has made me very happy too," as she blinked back the tears.

They both knew that the other was thinking of the many hours John had spent taking care of Christina and sharing many hours and days of entertainment while she was growing up.

Introductions complete. Papa said, "I'm taking everyone to dinner. We don't want to go home and cook now."

They all got into Dan's big car and were off to dinner.

At home John and Rachel, Dan and Chris sat long into the night talking about their family, when they were young, how they loved their papa and mother. How they rode together. Their life had been very full and mostly happy. Although it was hard at times because so much of what John and Christina had experienced in their youth, Brian was always there too. They both had thoughts, but neither said anything.

John said "I am so glad you two found each other. You seem perfect together."

"Thanks John, I'm glad I found her too," Dan said and Chris shook her head yes and smiled and squeezed Dan's hand.

"But Dan, she was a spicy little girl until she was about six. After that she was still energetic, but a little more gentle."

Dan responded, "She probably had to, surrounded by all you boys."

"That's why," Chris offered and laughed.

"But when she was born I felt responsible for her and took her under my wing and that lasted until I went to graduate school. I helped mom with her and mom taught me things about a baby and how to handle her. I felt important."

"That is why you're so good with the girls, you had a lot of practice with Chris," Rachel said.

"Katie is just like her," he said to Rachel and all.

"Yeah, there were lots of things he would not let me do," Chris interrupted.

"But you survived. Dan, look at Katie and you know Christina at that age."

"John, I loved the attention you gave me, not that Mother and Papa didn't, but I could always pop in your room and talk."

Papa added to the conversation, "Yeah, Lydia and I watched that and we were glad because there was eight years difference and they could have grown up hardly knowing each other. We loved it that John was her caretaker and took so much interest in her."

John thought about the day he came home and found Chris and Brian in the library. It was a surprise. After that it was not just Christina that I took places but Brian too. It was different at first, but finally I accepted him and felt I really had to look after her. I knew what boys did to girls, not my sister! At least he was not some older guy, but just a kid like she was.

John also told the family that he would probably be transferred to New Orleans by late summer. "If it happens I'm going to try to get there before school starts." John works for an oil company.

"We'll be a little closer, especially to Dave and Jim."

"About the same distance as Bill is from here. Hopefully you can come to visit more often," Papa said.

"Yeah, I'm glad about that, for a while I thought that I would be assigned overseas. And probably will later."

The evening had been long, but it had been just wonderful sitting around talking and getting to know Dan and sharing all the news that they all knew. The girls had gone to bed earlier and now the adults, all tired decided to do the same.

As John and Rachel lay close they talked about how glad they were that both Dan and Chris had chosen well.

"You remember how devastated we all were when Brian died, but you know I had so much sorrow for Chris I could hardly stand it. It's obvious she and Dan love each other very much. He seems to fit in well and he is a pretty nice looking guy with a great career," John said.

"He really is."

In his childhood bedroom it was quiet and the day had been long, they fell asleep with contentment in their hearts.

♥

It was Tuesday and everybody got up and slowly met the day. After lunch everyone except papa dawned heavy coats, hats, gloves and went for a long walk. It was rather cold but not much snow.

"It is such a change from the city. The peace and tranquility overwhelms me. I forget when I'm gone, but it all comes back to me with such ease," John said.

"Yeah, from where I live and work in the city, then come out here. I know what you mean." Dan added, "You guys were very fortunate to grow up in such a beautiful spot."

"We move around so often, but always in a city, I feel bad sometimes Julie and Katie will never know what we all had."

"They are certainly enjoying it now." Dan responded as they watched the dogs chase the girls then the girls chase the dogs.

"Maybe if Papa is okay with it they can come out this summer for a while. If we move before school starts maybe they can stay with him during the move."

"We'll be close and could look in on them."

Rachel asked Chris, "What time do we expect Karen and Bill?"

"Karen said around four. Bill had to take a quick trip to work so they would be a little late starting," Chris answered. "Dan is so looking forward to seeing Bill again. They have talked on the phone a few times. He still isn't over how this all worked out."

"When do you want to start dinner?" Rachel asked Chris.

"Probably three will be soon enough."

On the way back to the house the guys walked ahead and were in deep conversation about oil and photography.

Inside they all warmed up in front of the fireplace. Soon Chris and Rachel went to the kitchen to prepare the dinner. Dan came in and said he would get the table ready. Chris showed him where to find the dishes and she went back to the kitchen.

"Oh Chris he is so sweet."

"I think so. From day one he has been so considerate."

While they were busy the dogs, as they always do, sensed a strange car in the driveway. Daisy ran to the big window and with her bark confirmed.

"Dan get your coat. Bill and Karen are here."

Quickly Dan had his coat on and they were out to greet the Pittsburgh Zellers. Bill jumped out and almost ran to Dan and they hugged and patted each other on the back, hugged some more.

"Can you believe meeting again like this?"

"Can you believe I'm marrying your sister? Who would have thought? I believe you got taller."

"You too. We were boys then. How did you find us again?"

"Timing was so perfect. When I came out to get her for dinner, I knew—I knew I had been here before. It slowly came back."

"So much has happened in these years, but it seems like yesterday. It's all the greatest," Bill said.

"Why did we come out here?" Dan asked

"Not sure I remember."

"I saw Chris and her German shepherds."

"They were truly her dogs. Usually the dog sleeps with the kid, well it was the other way around, Chris would sleep with them."

Karen, the girls and their little dog got out and after hugs they watched the show of what seemed to be a greeting of old friends. They were so delighted to meet again they almost cried.

Karen and Chris laughed at both of them until they almost cried.

"I bet Bill said, 'I can hardly wait,' a dozen times, coming over."

Finally Bill and Dan gave up and Bill hugged his sister.

"Come meet the three loves of my life, Karen, Emily and Lisa."

Dan took Karen's hand and kissed her lightly on the cheek. "It couldn't be more wonderful. And this is Lisa and Emily?" He took their little hands and said, "I'm so glad to know you young ladies." They danced around.

"And this is Sally," Emily said as she pointed to her little white dog on a leash.

"I'm six and Lisa is five."

Chris said, "We'd better go in."

"Who's here?" Bill asked Chris.

"Just John and Rachel and the girls. The others are coming up tomorrow."

Inside and after all the greetings were over they all relaxed with a glass of wine and soon dinner was served.

♥

The next day the St. Louis Zellers arrived in Jim's van. Again Dan and Chris went out to meet them along with the dogs. Out jumped five little children who were more interested in the dogs than people. But soon they hugged their Aunt Christina and were presented to their new Uncle Dan.

Dave and Jim first told Dan how happy they were to meet him and welcome him to the family. Chris received hugs and kisses too. The girls too welcomed Dan and he greeted them in his warm and loving way. They all went in and hugged their papa and the other family members. It was a festive afternoon. Julie and Katie took charge of their little cousins as they got reacquainted.

Later the girls prepared dinner. The guys gathered in the library and caught up on everything that everyone was doing. John about New Orleans. Dave would start working on his doctorate next year. Dan and Chris were probably going to Paris for a month to work, not a vacation. Jim who worked for IBM knew computer science was the new frontier.

Dan slipped out to check with Chris, was there anything that he could do. The table. She assured him that the girls would relieve him of that duty tonight. But he could get the wine.

As Bill and Dan went to the wine cellar they continued their happiness together.

"I'm watching for an opening in Chicago. Then we could be closer. There is a hugh research and development on the south side of the city. You and Chris are still going to live there?"

"That would be great. Yeah it is a great agency to work for. Although I'll still have to travel some. But I'm taking her with me. She has been alone too long and so have I."

"Papa is going to be alone again," Bill said.

"We'll probably be out here on weekends. He and Ellen do things together. And he is over at the Grange a lot and he still does some consulting and goes to lunch with friends. From what Chris says, he is quite busy."

"He and Ellen share things, but I would be surprised if he ever marries again. He loved our mother so very much. He was openly affectionate toward her, especially at home. He would kiss her, they would hold hands, bring her flowers for no special occasion."

"He seems content, and he talks about her often, not in a sad way but in a special way, that she was a part of his life and still is. One day he had brought flowers home and said, 'these are for Lydia if she were here.' I almost feel guilty taking Chris away from him."

"No don't, she deserves you and she too has a life of her choosing."

"I wasn't sure there for a while," Dan said.

Dan briefly told Bill what had happened that Saturday.

"Oh my god, I'm so glad you were persistent. We all knew and were afraid that she would never get over what happened. For two years every time I talked to papa I ask him, if Chris was dating anyone. The answer was always no. Finally one day he said, I think so and do you remember Dan Halloran. I said no. And then he helped me recall and it all came back to me and I almost fell off my chair."

"But now everything is right with us," Dan assured him.

"You'll never know how glad we all are that she found her way," and Bill shook his head.

"Thanks, I'm glad too."

"We're supposed to be getting wine. Let's get three of each, red and white. Papa has this marked, DINNER WINE". They selected and returned to the kitchen, trying to stay out of the girl's way as they opened the bottles and placed them on the dining table.

After dinner they all sat around talking and catching up on what the others had been doing. It was rare that everyone would be here at the same time. They all relished the time together and to welcome their new brother–in–law. They all seemed to like and approve of him. Dan was easy to be with and easy to love. Everyone here, Dan could see what Christina meant when she referred to a full house.

Papa showed his grandchildren their Christmas tree with all the toy ornaments. They had seen them before but being younger had forgotten about them. Several of them would be expecting Santa and the others giggled because they knew.

After everyone had retired for the night Chris, Dan and Bill got the house and dogs, all three, ready for the night.

"Good night you two," Bill said as he went to be with Karen.

Dan and Chris went to their bedroom and showered and fell into bed exhausted. "I can't believe how you have managed this bunch the last four days. You did all the cooking, getting everyone organized. Helping the children. I'm overwhelmed just watching you."

"Oh I had a lot of help. I just kind of told everybody what they could do."

"But you organized all the food and you got it done."

"But you and Bill got the wine," and she giggled.

"Oh gosh," Dan couldn't resist.

"Well, I was in high school when all the guys started coming home with their families and mother taught me well."

"I would have loved to have known your mother."

"I still miss her and so wish she could be here for our special day."

Chris and Dan snuggled close and continued a few more words, then easily fell asleep in each other's arms.

♥

The next morning Papa Zeller, Christina and the boys went to visit their mother's grave. It was an intimate time for her beloved husband and children. The air was crisp and fresh with the clouds and sun vying for a place in the winter sky. A soft layer of snow covered her grave like a shroud.

They took poinsettias, holly berries and evergreens to adorn her resting place. The contrast of red flowers and berries and greens against the white of the snow made a perfect picture that was borne out of love for this dear lady. She would have approved.

She had been so important to all of them and they wanted to show their love for her was still very strong and how much they missed her. This was their only way.

They walked around remembering happy moments with her, remembering little things special to each one of them. Of course they all had many, but one they all remembered was the day she brought Christina home from the hospital and she was not a boy.

Their mother explained that she was their new baby sister, a girl, different from you boys. The understanding spanned from, yes mom I know, to confusion, I really don't quite know what you are talking about.

Papa remembered how beautiful she had been on their wedding day. Christina was a little surprised he mentioned their wedding day. Does he know? She thought.

Bill offered, "How she could manage us when we were out of order, yet be so caring at the same time. She could get us to behave and you didn't even know you were doing it. All done with soft voice and loving words."

"So many years have passed without her," Papa Zeller said. "And yet it seems like yesterday that we all came here but we had to go away and leave her behind. But enough, we have a special event and it will be pure happiness."

With those last words they all got back in Jim's van and made their way home.

♥

At home things were a little quieter and at lunch Chris and Dan announced they wanted to take pictures of all the children. "Chris will be in charge of posing and I will do the camera," Dan said.

"This will be a come–as–you–are–session," Chris announced. "Do you want to take them in the hall underneath the family gallery," she asked Dan.

"Yes," and he looked at her remembering.

After lunch, everyone went upstairs to watch this performance and Dan got all set up.

"This is going to be fun with you in charge."

Christina gathered all of her little nieces and nephews around and told them what she wanted them to do.

"We're going to start with Lisa and listen very carefully what I ask her to do, because I will be asking everyone to do about the same thing."

Chris helped Lisa on the bench, "Now Lisa think about ice cream, I want an expression." She explained what expression meant to the little ones. "Now look happy, Santa Clause—what about a surprise—now something you shouldn't have done and dad found out—look like someone took your candy—now laugh—daddy just came home from work."

275

Chris and Dan took all of the pictures in that manner. It was a fun time for moms and dads to watch and smile.

"Get your papa and have him sit on the bench and gather all the children around him." Papa was among those watching and willingly obliged.

"That will be a nice ending," Dan said to Bill who was standing close. "I don't take portraits of children but this has been so much fun. It was Chris' idea. I think I'll hire her. We'll make a folio for everybody."

Bill asked Dan, "Did you see young Jim's expression when Chris said Santa Clause."

"No I didn't."

"He raised his eye brows and puffed out his cheeks and you could tell what he was thinking."

"An eight year old, he knows and that is probably why Chris didn't mention Santa to the older ones. She knows too."

"This was great, what a nice memory," Bill said.

Later Dave, Jim and their wives went out to get some last minute things.

Bill and Dan played several games of pool as Karen and Chris sat by and chatted. All of the children were under their care as they were busy with toys, dogs or just napping. Otherwise the remainder of the afternoon passed rather quietly

Then there was dinner to prepare all over again. The girls decided that they should all eat in the kitchen this time. Chris didn't object. Dinner over they started to prepare the dining table for the Christmas Eve dinner.

Another long day was about to close and excitement for the bigger day to come was on everybody's mind.

♥

At last it was Christmas Eve. The florist came early and decorated the library and the dining table with red and white roses, holly, greens and candles that Dan and Chris had chosen.

In the early afternoon the phone rang. Expecting a call from his family Dan answered, "Zellers."

"Could I please speak to Dan?"

"Hi Dad."

"It sounded like you but I know her brothers are all there. We're at the hotel. We came with Jake. What do we do?"

"Well Chris is planning dinner at six. So come over around four and as I told mom, it's a dressy occasion."

"She remembered. Also mom wants to know if Chris needs help."

"No she has hired two ladies to prepare dinner so all of us can enjoy the evening. But dad you wouldn't believe how she has handled this bunch. Just be prepared, the house is full and many little children and three dogs. See you at four."

Near four o'clock Dan's family arrived as well as Ellen and Jan. Ellen being a family friend knew all the boys. Jan had met Bill, Dave and their families before, but there needed to be a few more introductions.

Everyone was dressed and cocktails were served and then dinner. Christina again had made little place cards for seating, Santa's for the children and white doves for adults. Papa Zeller would be at one end and Dan at the other, just like Thanksgiving.

When dinner was over Papa Zeller tapped his glass and everyone quieted and looked his way. He rose and said, "I have a few words," and he paused. "To Dan, from me and all my sons and their family we welcome you into this family with open arms. Dan you'll never know how happy you have made all of us especially Christina. I know you love her more than you even know. We have all been together this week and you melded into this wild and crazy bunch seamlessly. It's like you have been here forever. We're ecstatic that you and Christina found each other. And with love in our hearts a big, big welcome." He smiled happily over the family and sat down.

And he wanted to say how much he wished Christina's mother could be here to see her only daughter so happy, but he did not. It would send a pall of sadness into these happy moments.

Dan too wanted to say a few words and with a tap on his glass the attention was directed his way. "Thank you John, with much love I accept your gracious words and their meaning. It is so wonderful that we're all here together, family and friends, and to share our special occasion. When Chris and I were choosing a date she said she wanted all of her brothers to be here, so this time was an easy choice. She often told me how much fun she had growing up with all you guys."

278

He paused then continued, "You all have made me feel so welcome. To her papa and her brothers, I can easily say I love her more than I can express. I'll care for her and protect her for all of our days. That summer day when she introduced herself, I'm Christina Zeller, I felt sure that my search for a soul mate was over. It was and I never looked back. She has made me so very happy and I want to make her very happy as well," as he looked lovingly at her.

Dan continued, "To my mother and father. Thank you a million times over for the care and love you have given me through the years and helped me to become an adult. I love you both very much. And to my big brother, helping with those delicate moments that one faces when you are young," and they both smiled and silently reminiscing of those personal times that Jake had explained things to Dan.

Dan looked back at Chris and said, "I must confess, that Monday I called and said I forgot my notebook, well I didn't," and he reached for her hand, "Well I just couldn't wait until evening to see you again."

She smiled and looked surprised and said softly, "You didn't."

"One last comment I couldn't be happier to be the chosen one to complete this family. But we intend to expand by more than just me. Love you everyone." Of course everyone smiled and laughed softly, even the little children although they did not exactly know why.

After dinner the adults exchanged gifts and enjoyed Christmas Eve to the utmost. The evening over Dan went back to Le Chateau with his family.

279

♥

Christmas morning the little children were up early to see what Santa had brought them. Dave's little girl had expressed concern, would Santa know they were all here at their papa's. But it seems that he found all of them just fine. It was a busy hour.

The next excitement of the day was Aunt Christina's wedding. Papa and John were ready early to receive those coming for the ceremony. There was a small string ensemble from school and they would play before and after. Jeremy, the music teacher from school and friend of Christina's, would be the vocalist. Dan's friend, Steve, would do the photographing. The minister, and of course Dan and his family, Aunt Mary, Uncle Edward and cousins of Christina.

Upstairs was the busiest place of all. Everyone was getting dressed. Everything slowly fell into place and with soft strings singing throughout the house, Christina came down the spiral staircase to her waiting papa.

When Papa Zeller saw her he gasps lightly.

Softly he said, "Lydia," and his eyes became heavy.

"You remembered," she softly answered back.

"Oh honey, you never forget your wedding day. You didn't tell me."

"I wanted to surprise you. It is a part of mother that can be here."

The beautiful dress that Christina's mother wore so long ago and now Christina, is ivory silk velvet and she especially liked the French lace that covers the fitted bodice and long sleeves. Her necklace was a gold heart with a diamond in the center and matching earrings that Dan had given her. She carried a small bouquet of red rosebuds, baby's breath and greens.

"Everything is so perfect and you are as beautiful as she was. I wish you as much peace and love as we had," he said lovingly to his only daughter.

The family all in formal attire made their way to the elegantly decorated library. Dave's young son received the honor of carrying the pillow that held their wedding bands. All of the little boys were dressed in navy pants and winter white jackets. The girls all seemed proud to be in their long ivory colored dresses, so much like their Aunt Christina's. Jan's dress was deep red and also silk velvet, and last Christina with her beloved papa.

Dan and all were waiting in the beautifully decorated library. His heart danced when he saw her and broke into a captivating and most contented smile that she had ever seen on his happy face. She kissed her papa and softly said, "But I will always love you too."

Tears welled up in papa's eyes and a million memories passed through his mind. My little girl. My little girl how I love her back. He placed her hand in Dan's and enclosed them both in his and softly, "God bless you dear children and I wish you peace and love all the day to come."

She stepped beside Dan and all the words to be man and wife were exchanged. They looked into each other's eyes and said their vows so softly that only the other could hear. They were words for each other and only each other.

Jeremy then sang a prayer accompanied by flute and oboe. Happy tears and smiles were on every face especially her brother John.

Chris and Dan stood for moments smiling at each other and they seemed to be far away, far away together. One lonely tear trickled down her cheek and Dan tenderly kissed it away. Then they reached for each other and their lips met in a gentle and loving way.

After the ceremony everyone lingered for pictures and just to express happiness. In time they all went to the reception. As they arrived Chris and Dan were met by her students and they nearly swept her away. Many friends and family of both were there to help them celebrate. Dinner, dancing, talking and the evening was long but they wanted to stay and enjoy everyone because it would probably be a while until they saw many of them again.

When the evening was over Christina kissed her papa and all of her brothers and said, "See you at home tomorrow."

Dan and Chris went to the bridal suite and he carried her over the threshold and put her down and slowly closed the door.

"A heavy heart, Beloved, have I borne
From year to year until I saw thy face."

♥

ACKNOWLEDGMENTS

Life itself must be acknowledged as part of the creative spirit.

Individually, to the poets whose words are timeless and reached our hearts, especially those remembered in this book, Robert Burns, Omar Khayyam, Sidney Lanier, and Elizabeth Barrett Browning.

The tool of music that helped me reach into a greater realm of imagination and bring forth words that otherwise might have been lost.

To family and friends through the years, have all in some way left a mark that I remember often.

To my husband Joe, a love that was spread over the many years together.

To my sons, David and Joseph, I found a love that I never knew existed until they graced my life. And Jill my daughter-in-law added a beautiful dimension to that love.

To my editor, Nina Alveraz, who helped me fine-tune this work of fiction. Her help was invaluable.

Lastly, but as important, Bridgette first, Freddy, Holly and Max later, and others, I found their innocent wisdom very fulfilling. Hopefully, I have made their lives as wonderful as they have made mine.

The author lives with her family and dogs in upstate New York

www.ingramcontent.com/pod-product-compliance
Lightning Source LLC
Chambersburg PA
CBHW071300170626
46809CB00001B/297